SUPERVILLAINOUS!

SUPERVILLAINOUS!

Confessions of a Costumed Evil-doer

By Mike Leon

A Createspace book

Cover art by Bill Owen

PLEASE SEND ALL COMMENTS, QUESTIONS AND DEATH THREATS TO:

PROFESSIONAL.MIKE.LEON@GMAIL.COM

To Lloyd Kaufman, for inspiring me to write something truly ridiculous.

FORELUORD

When I was a little boy, plastic superhero figures with kung fu action and spring loaded missiles were a fixture in my house. I looked to comics and cartoons about super powered individuals with an almost biblical reverence. Whenever my stay at home mother took me out shopping for groceries or shoes I would look to the skies hoping for a glimpse of General Welfare or the Scarlet Avenger as they dazzled through the clouds on their way to do battle with the agents of evil. Unfortunately for me, not much super-heroing goes on in southern Ohio (for reasons I learned much later, during the writing of this very book).

As I got older and the other kids became less interested in superpowered saviors and more interested in mundane things like sports and girls, I remained infatuated, even occasionally obsessed. I went through many of the normal phases of geeky adolescence. I did a stint playing dungeons and dragons. I tried my hand at comic book art (don't even ask to see the drawings – they're hideous). It was in my late teens I discovered I had a talent for writing with some early attempts at superhero fantasy novels. It was some of that early work that caught the attention of my first publisher and it was they who recommended me to Weird World magazine and that work which got me noticed for my first novel deal and that novel deal that got me my first agent and so on and so on. So I can pretty easily say it is because of superheroes that I do what I do now. I can also easily say superheroes are why I did not have sex with a girl until I was twenty one.

That aside, when my agent of the last five years, Larry Greenberg, asked me if I would interview a supervillain for Trigger magazine I jumped at the chance. I would learn later that, despite Larry's insistence that I was his first choice for the job, he had actually been to eight other writers who turned him down (except one who quit after he was nearly crushed by a giant robot upon arriving for the initial interview). The way I see it, it's their loss – not mine.

I jumped at the assignment so quickly that I didn't even bother to ask what supervillain I would be interviewing. I figured with a magazine as high profile as Trigger they would be sending me to talk to Reverend Endtimes or El Malo Grande (then chairman of the Global Crime League). I could not have been more wrong.

I was only vaguely familiar with Hammerspace (the villain and the unusual metaphysical fantasy construct from which he derives his name). I didn't know who he was or what he would become. I'll even admit I was a little disappointed when Larry told me about him. Why would Trigger want an interview with a C list supervillain? Larry's answer, as always, was standard industry fluff – the guy was really on the way up. What he really meant was that they wanted a higher profile villain but couldn't get one and the magazine still needed to fill the space. I briefly considered dumping the assignment at that point. I thought it might be a mistake to associate myself and my career with such a potentially embarrassing throwaway article about a nobody whacko who wears a costume to work.

I know now that Trigger had made the only mistake. They had grossly underestimated the man that would become a legend. They had misjudged the situation entirely. I remember calling Larry Greenberg the first night of the project and telling him there was much more there than a four page spread between cologne ads. There was a whole book there. This is that book.

I hope that with this book you can gain what I did – a truly intimate view inside the world of the costumed crusaders who protect us and the superpowered archenemies who attempt to enslave that world on a daily basis. Perhaps you can learn a little bit more about the impetus that drives a man to throw down his wrench, walk out on his factory job, put on orange tights and start building a doomsday laser. Maybe this book will help you find some answers to your questions on the deeper meaning of that great battle between good and evil. Hell, even if it does none of that, I hope you'll at least find it entertaining.

CHAPTER ONE

It's almost noon as Hammerspace walks into a Dunkin Donuts on the I-95 for our interview. I can't help but think the up and coming supervillain is as far from cliché as a supervillain can get as he sits down across from me in his purple rubberized armor and black trench coat. He doesn't wear a shred of spandex and a cape is nowhere to be seen.

"A lot of guys dropped the cape back in the late nineties. It just went out. And you can't blame them really. You ever try to ride a motorcycle with one of those things? It's a real good way to end up like Isadora Duncan. Of course I catch a lot of flak for the black trench coat. It used to just be sort of roguish. Highlander wore a black trench coat. After Columbine it has a whole other meaning, but I didn't become a professional evil-doer to worry about hurting people's feelings."

Is that what you call it? Professional evil-doing?

"Well, that's a little long winded. I'm a big fan of

what works. Supervillain. Supervillainy. Criminal enterprise. Evil mastermind is a good one."

Hammerspace obviously isn't shy about his moral alignment. "Why would I be?" He says as he sips a black coffee from a paper cup. "With the kind of nonsense that goes on in the world every day, I think it's refreshing to have some people that just say 'Hey, look, we're evil. We're the bad guys.' I mean look at the last three presidents of the United States. Clinton promised to fix the economy, but he just wanted to run the show and get his knob polished. Bush was all hometown, God and country, but he just wanted to run the show and kill some towel heads. Then there was Obama, all about hope and change, but he really just wanted to run the show and, who knows, healthcare, something, something, socialism. This new guy – who knows, but I'm sure it's the same. At least I'm not covering anything. I want to rule the world. Bam. There it is. It's on the table. That's it. No bullshit. And I'm better than those guys because of it."

And he may be on to something. After two recent high profile scuffs with New York's most prominent superhero, Hammerspace most definitely has some idea what he's talking about, even if he is a little cocky. "General Welfare is a fool, a pathetic fool and I will crush him and enslave his beloved city."

Of course being a super powered scoundrel has left a bad taste in the mouths of some. The mayor's office officially labeled Hammerspace a threat to public safety last month after his most recent bout with General Welfare, in which a subway train was completely destroyed and a young woman was witnessed falling hundreds of feet from a skyscraper before being swept to safety by the military uniformed protector of freedom. "I said 'You may have defeated me this time, Welfare, but can you defeat gravity itself to save the woman you love?' and I threw the bitch off the building. How classic is that?"

Hammerspace chuckles as he takes a bite from a donut with cherry filling. He appears surprised and puts the donut down to curse at the donut shop clerk. The clerk looks like he's not sure whether to call the police or look for a hidden camera. I defuse the situation by asking the next question.

"What is it that makes me a super villain and not just a villain? I have a super power. I mean, obviously." I inquire further. "Christ, you're not too keen on the research part of your job are you?" I explain to him that the question is just for the purpose of the interview because people want to read these things coming straight from him. He gets it. "Well, it's like this: I can keep anything in my jacket. Whatever it is, I can toss it in there and pull it back out later. It doesn't necessarily have to fit underneath the coat, as long as I can fit it in there initially." What he means is that he has a magic satchel, as it is called in the literary world. In the early nineteen hundreds, with the advent of animation, cartoon characters, who weren't limited by the laws of physics like live actors were, began to pull all kinds of objects seemingly from the nowhere around them; baseball bats, guns, musical instruments, anvils and, last but most certainly not least, giant mallets. This led to the coinage of the term hammerspace – a word for the extra dimension from which all of these objects were drawn. When Bugs Bunny pulls out a huge mallet and uses it to smash

Elmer Fudd, he is pulling that mallet out of his hammerspace.

"Yeah. It comes from old cartoons. It's sort of an obscure word so I figured you would have to be kind of smart to get it and those are the best kind. It's the clever little names you have to think about for a second that you remember. Some guys just don't get these things at all. I worked with a villain last year called Deathkiller. That's trying too hard. It sounds like a high school thrash metal band. We get it already. He's evil. Whatever. He ended up getting shot by his own remote control nerve poison dart gun. Beginner mistake. It didn't surprise anybody. Speaking of poison there's a guy that works for ▉▉▉▉ called the Toxic Shocker. He even kind of looks like a tampon, but I met him once and he's more of a douche than anything. Then there's Dick Detective, do what you want with that one. Saikoziz, because apparently being too dumb to spell is cool. Commander Commando wants us to know he's really commanding I guess." I try to skew the conversation back to the actual physics of his super ability but he really likes this topic (and honestly I find it too insightful to exclude – I hope no one mentioned is offended). "Then you have the guys with names that just don't make sense. The Black Bandit is a white guy. I think maybe that makes him racist, but I'm not exactly sure. General Welfare's sidekick's name is Jose Canyousee. It sounds clever at first, but then you meet the kid and you realize it wasn't intentional. And the titles are all over the place. Everybody's Doctor this or Captain that. Captain Colonics is my favorite. That guy is way too into holistic medicine. I thought about a title for a while but I couldn't come up with one that had a good sound to it."

About five minutes later he finally stops talking about how easy it is to get a lordship outside of Great Britain and we get back to the subject of his jacket. He explains that he doesn't necessarily have to be wearing a jacket, but that he just needs some sort of fold or pocket (something I didn't know going into the interview). He lists some items he commonly carries around. "Hand grenades, ray guns, and of course the Mallet of Malice." The Mallet of Malice is Hammerspace's trademark weapon. He draws the medieval warhammer from the jacket as he talks about it and sets it down on the table. "I got it at one of those festivals where a bunch of nerds dress up in fairy costumes and sell ten dollar turkey drumsticks. It's not magic or anything. I really don't even use it that much. I whip it out and wave it around to look cool, but if the shit really hits the fan with invincible super foes I need the heavy artillery, not some replica for forty year old guys that still live with their mom."

An hour later we're pounding the sidewalk. Hammerspace stops at a newspaper vending box to get a tabloid that features a tiny picture of him down in the corner. He puts a quarter in the machine but takes the entire stack once it's open. He drops all the tabloids along the sidewalk as we continue walking. Theft and littering before ten AM. The guy takes his evil-doing seriously. A busty girl gives us the stink eye as she passes and both of us give her a good once over. "You get really kooky women in this business," he says. "I was with this girl for a little while. She would crawl around naked on all fours and howl like a wolf around the house. It didn't work out. The suicide girl look is pretty much a necessity. I haven't been with a girl who didn't walk around in torn fishnets since my ex-wife. Normal women just don't go for the whole evil empire thing I guess – unless you're really successful. El Malo Grande can't go to the Quik Stop without taking a supermodel back to his volcano fortress. It's probably like that with any career really."

As he drops the last of the newspapers we're interrupted by a startlingly loud throat clearing sound. Behind us stands a bevy of costume clad personalities with their arms crossed and capes flowing. Superheroes.

CHAPTER TWO

Hammerspace rolls his eyes and frowns smugly as he takes in the costumed cadre before us. He sighs. This reporter is uncertain what to do, as there may be a dangerous super powered battle of titanic proportions about to explode before him.

The team of superheroes ahead of us is called The Five Freedoms and they wear star spangled jump suits that appear old and somewhat faded as if they may have picked through Evel Knievel's trash to form their wardrobe. Their leader, The Flouridian, speaks.

"So, um, Hammerspace, you're a wanted criminal," says The Flouridian in a shivering, uncertain voice. "We can't let you go."

Hammerspace replies with a sneer. "I don't have time for suposers. Get lost."

Suposers is a derogatory term for superheroes, specifically ones of questionable aptitude. "It's super and poser. You put the words together and you get suposer. Also known as spandies, costards, justies, super zeroes, vigilidiots, the list goes on and on," Hammerspace explains. "I wish you could see how much of this I deal with. People think that superpowers are always worth having, but that's because you only ever hear about the useful ones. For every General Welfare out there there's ten other guys who had the same lab accident but ended up with an ability to smell colors or turn gold into silver by touching it or pee orange juice or something else that's totally worthless. Most of them are smart enough to know they don't have anything going for them, but some of them end up like these idiots."

And he isn't exaggerating. The Five Freedoms consist of The Flouridian, a man whose teeth (and only his teeth) are completely invincible, The Lamanator, who has the miraculous ability to read the mind of Lorenzo Lamas from anywhere on the planet, The Tether, an inner city youth who can fly as long as some part of his body is touching the ground, Force Field Girl, a young woman who can turn invisible, and last but not least, Foursight, a jazz musician who only sees what will be happening four minutes in the future.

The following is a transcript taken from my tape recording of the event:

Flouridian: You can't talk about us like that, Hammerspace.

Hammerspace: I just did. What are you gonna do about it?

Foursight: Oh no, not Force Field Girl!

SUPERVILLAINOUS!

Force Field Girl: What? What about Force Field Girl?

Foursight: You get blown up after General Welfare gets here.

The Tether: General Welfare?

Foursight: He gets here but Hammerspace knows about it already somehow and he's ready for him.

Hammerspace: Mwa ha ha ha ha! You're a fool Foursight! You've brought doom upon yourself and your comrades! (Hammerspace pulls a large shovel from his jacket.)

Foursight: But General Welfare will be ready for you when he gets here. He already knows you know.

Hammerspace: Does he now? (Hammerspace pulls a hand grenade from his jacket.)

Flouridian: Foursight, shut up! You're going to get us all killed!

Force Field Girl: No! I have to know how I get blown up. I don't want to die!

Lamanator: Lorenzo has decided to change the style of his ponytail!

Flouridian: That's all he ever does! Why are you even on the team?

Mike Leon: Do you mind if I ask you some questions?

Flouridian: Identify yourself!

Mike Leon: Mike Leon, I'm interviewing Hammerspace for Trigger magazine. How long have you been superheroes?

Flouridian: Whoa! Whoa! We're not superheroes. That's a trademark. We're super heroes. Two words.

Mike Leon: I don't think that's how trademarks work.

Flouridian: Are you an intellectual property attorney?

Mike Leon: No.

Flouridian: Then shut up. You want to get sued?

Force Field Girl: Please don't let me die! Please!

Lamanator: Can't you just make a force field?

Force Field Girl: No. That's not my power!

The Tether: It's not? That's stupid.

Hammerspace: Enough! It's time for you all to meet your doom!

Hammerspace tosses the hand grenade into the

group of superheroes. I turn and leap head first into an open dumpster. The dumpster rattles from the blast of the grenade. I poke my head out in time to see Hammerspace smacking The Flouridian in the face with the Mallet of Malice. An invincible tooth embeds itself in the steel of the dumpster.

The Tether flies toward Hammerspace with one finger touching the ground, and the Lamanator comes at him with an uprooted stop sign (I'm still unsure if he plucked it himself or it was blown free by the grenade), but Hammerspace is like an engine of destruction amidst the feeble abilities of The Five Freedoms. He sends them sprawling. As the members of the hero team attempt to peel themselves from the pavement he cackles loudly.

"Your powers are useless against me, Freedoms," he says as he raises his mallet to crush the head of the unconscious Lamanator. "Now I shall destroy you all!"

But as Hammerspace brings the mallet down something stops him. Something none of us saw coming (well, except for Foursight) halts the force of his smashing attack with quickness like none I've ever seen before.

"Well, well, well, if it isn't Doctor Jacket causing mayhem and destruction," says the star spangled crusader before us in a booming and masculine voice reminiscent of a 1960's television commercial. He stands an even six feet of perfectly chiseled muscle decked out in a skin tight American flag themed costume topped by a four star general's M1 steel pot helmet. He is General Welfare, possibly the most well known superhero in the world.

"I can't let you hurt these citizens, Jacket!" Welfare thunderously proclaims as he lifts Hammerspace off the ground by his neck with one hand.

"For the tenth time at least, it's Hammerspace. Hammer space," Hammerspace angrily replies. "Now be a real patriot and DIE for your country!" As he shouts he draws a flame thrower and unleashes a furious stream of burning napalm that engulfs General Welfare. The General tosses Hammerspace to the ground.

"Only monsters settle their problems with guns, Jacket! It's a good thing I'm completely invulnerable or that cowardly cheap shot would have hurt."

"Blast you, Welfare! Mark my words! We will meet again!"

With that, Hammerspace tosses a smoke bomb at the ground and vanishes. He's gone. I bury myself back in the dumpster to avoid being seen by the recovering superheroes, but I've lost him. I've lost Hammerspace.

CHAPTER THREE

Melvin Mitchell Thompson, the boy who would become one of the world's greatest supervillains was born in Flint, Michigan, a little town right smack in the middle of the glove. Throughout the middle of the twentieth century the city was a thriving industrial complex. Flint was the original headquarters of General Motors near the beginning of the century and continued to be one of the largest centers of automobile production even after the leaders of the company moved to Detroit. During the Second World War a large portion of allied tanks and vehicles were manufactured in Flint. After the war, Flint continued to produce thousands of cars well into the nineteen sixties when the city began a slow decline. It began with the cultural phenomenon popularly referred to as "white flight" and worsened during the seventies oil crisis. With automobile sales at record lows due to skyrocketing oil prices, production was cut. Lower production meant lower employment, and to the city of Flint that meant grave news. Auto workers, a huge portion of the city's residents, began losing jobs. Local businesses began to lose revenue. A chain reaction had begun that would climax with the closing of nearly all the GM plants in Flint and the departure of almost everyone who could afford to leave. By nineteen-ninety, Flint was a rotting carcass of drug addicts and die hard American auto workers who simply refused to leave even after years of unemployment.

"I was about ten when the plant closed and I was about fifteen when I think my dad finally realized things weren't going to get better" says Hammerspace while standing in front of the Flint Cultural Center. "It took him years. He just kept saying they were going to come back. I don't know what he was thinking. It's like he thought all the Japanese cars were just going to catch fire one day and everyone would start buying American again. I don't know."

After the better part of a decade without income, unable to provide for his family, Melvin's father, Jackson Thompson, strangled himself to death with his bare hands in one of the most bizarre suicides on record. "Anyone who says it's not possible didn't meet my old man. The bastard was tough. All those old factory guys were," Hammerspace recounts. "It took the cops weeks to figure out how he did it."

Melvin's mother, Irina Thompson, employed part time at the local Betamax manufacturing facility, struggled to make ends meet. In 1991 the plant closed. Financially destitute, Melvin's mother attempted to turn to prostitution. "She must have been terrible in the sack," he explains. "I just remember her apologizing a lot and offering refunds. She ended up feeling bad for a lot of guys and giving them back more than they paid. It was no way to conduct business."

By the time Melvin was eighteen the situation had become dire. Unable to afford food, the Thompsons had regressed to eating the roaches that infested the family home. After a time without any food in the house, even the roaches left. It was then that Melvin took matters into his own hands. He went into town one afternoon wearing his best shoes and his best shirt and began entering local businesses to inform them that he would do absolutely anything for a paycheck. After hours of scouring Melvin entered the Little Caesar's Pizza on Main Street in downtown Flint.

"I was taking a pie off the oven when this kid walks in," Tony Giacomo, the store manager at the time, retells. "I felt bad for him is all. I nailed his mom a week before and came out five bucks ahead and you know it's bad when it comes to that." Feeling sorry for Melvin, Tony Giacomo offered him the only job he had available. "Back then we had just got those low flush toilets, and this was during the cheeser cheeser days, so you wouldn't believe the monster number twos that was going into those shitters. Thing is, the hardware store went out of business and this was before the internet. We were all working ninety hours a week and none of us was going to drive to Detroit to get a plunger. So the toilets were plugged up all the time and you just had to man up and reach down there. I didn't have time for it, but I couldn't get nobody else onto the payroll neither. So I told him, I says every turd you pull out, I'll give you a dollar under the table. He was happier than a pig in shit."

Melvin set to work that very day. He was arguably the best toilet unclogger the Little Caesar's pizza chain ever employed. "There wasn't a minute went by that kid didn't have his hand down a toilet," Giacomo recounts. "He was the hardest worker I ever seen. He pulled ten, fifteen, twenty turds a day. After a few months one of my guys lost a hand in a pizza cutter mishap and got laid off so I gave Melvin his place on the crew tossing pies. But he kept pulling turds too. That was back before all this hand washing bullshit. You can't do that now."

Melvin began working constantly at the pizza parlor. "I remember one week I worked one hundred seventy five hours. I just didn't sleep." With his extra earnings his mother was able to quit hooking. After she quit, the family found they had even more money coming in. With that money Irina could afford to buy Melvin's younger siblings cheap microwaveable macaroni and cheese. They tried it for a week, but then returned to eating roaches.

Things were looking up for the Thompson family by the mid nineteen nineties. Melvin was able to keep up with the mortgage on the family home and even Irina Thompson found a new job molding tapes at the local VHS plant. But working such long hours was beginning to take its toll on Melvin Thompson. "I barely remember the whole two year span from ninety two to ninety four. It's just a huge blur like a bad drug trip or something. Then she walked in one day and changed everything."

CHAPTER FOUR

"I just remember I was standing near the cash register and the store was pretty slow, it was a Sunday afternoon I think, and she comes walking in wearing her Birkenstocks and a peace sign shirt and she plops these brochures down on the counter and says I should join Greenpeace."

The aforementioned 'she' was Linda Sherman, 18, environmental advocate and future Ex-Mrs. Melvin Thompson. While he was initially dumbfounded by her pushy and domineering approach, she managed to recruit him to her cause by means he isn't shy describing nearly two decades later. "I banged her in the walk-in right there. It was my first time. A girl does something like that and what teenage guy wouldn't go with her to the ends of the earth?"

So Melvin quit his job and ran off with Linda on the journey that would change his life and the future of the world for years to come. Together they set sail on the Gaia's Child, an anti-whaling ship that toured the Pacific. Hammerspace elaborates. "I had put a little money together, and with my mom doing the tape gig and me gone she could rent out my room and make ends meet."

Aboard the Gaia's Child, life was an adventure for Melvin "We would pull up and just throw things at these little Japanese guys who were trying to kill dolphins. I know it was supposed to be a whaling thing, but it was usually dolphins for some reason," he recalls. "I didn't really care so much what it was about. I just knew we were having a good time throwing things at foreigners and having sex, holy crap, the sex. You wouldn't guess it anymore but she was just an animal in the sack back then. The girl was a total whore."

Unfortunately, Linda's insatiable sexual appetite was also the cause of intense drama on the ship. She cheated on Melvin with at least two shipmates onboard, and he suspects she was unfaithful on numerous single instances while the ship was in port. "I was in a bunch of fistfights over her," he says. "When you're a kid you don't realize women like that just aren't worth it. They don't care about you. She didn't care about me."

So it wasn't unusual for the couple to be squabbling in August of 1996 when the Gaia's Child, following a radar signal they suspected belonged to an undeclared whaling vessel, sailed straight into the accident that would leave Melvin with his unique ability to hide objects of any size on his person. "We came up on this ship that was just floating there in the middle of international waters and they weren't responding. Nobody knew what was going on. We figured they were just pulling some scam to make us go away," he says of that fateful day. "A lot of ships would sort of turn out the lights and just pretend they weren't home. That's not unheard of out there."

Melvin and Linda had begun an argument earlier that day, with her claiming that he did not actually care about their cause on the ship. "She said I was just in it to play around, and she was right, but I wasn't going to tell her she was right. You never tell a woman she's right. That was one thing I knew back then that I was actually right about," he says. So as the Gaia's Child dropped anchor and crewmen attempted to identify the unknown vessel before them, Melvin lowered a dingy to the surface and headed over to the ship against the wishes of the captain, in a daring gambit to prove his worthiness to Linda. "How was I supposed to know they were testing a sigma ray bomb?"

The sigma ray bomb was born out of a cold war era attempt to bring science fiction into science nonfiction. It was a bomb which, upon detonation, bathed the surrounding area with sigma rays, beams which leading scientists of the day theorized would freeze any moving objects in a form of stasis, allowing troops to move in and occupy an area without sustaining or inflicting any casualties. Unfortunately, the sigma ray bomb didn't pan out as planned. "We finally got it to work about ten years later but the carbon emissions were off the charts and we ended up getting slapped with a ton of violations," explains former Sgt. Raymond Holleran of military research and development. "In the end it was cheaper and way more environmentally friendly just to kill people, so we stuck with conventional explosives."

While the exact nature of the experiment in the Pacific isn't known to the public the details aren't important to Hammerspace. "I drove a boat into an army test target," he says of the event. "They dropped an experimental super science bomb on me. It happens."

Onlookers were less casual. "Aye, we figured the lass for dead, we did. Sunken straight to the bottom of Davy Jones's locker," recalls Captain Andre 'Peg Leg' Pilleggi, captain of the Gaia's Child at the time of the incident. "We looked over the starboard and seen that ghost ship light up like the armor of the valkyries. We turned about the port and were heading out on all engines when they spotted the crazy swabbie coming back."

"I was a little disoriented, but that was it," Hammerspace later told us. "Kind of like vertigo or something. You know when you see one of those Omnimax movies and there's that tunnel of colored lights at the beginning and you feel like you're going to fall out of your chair into the vastness of space? It was like that. That's what it's like to get superpowers. Of course I didn't know I had superpowers until much later."

After the accident, Linda didn't cheat on Melvin ever again. She took up knitting and insisted they settle on dry land. She picked out an apartment in Greenwich Village with money from her trust fund where she and Melvin lived for most of their early twenties. He took a job at a nearby standardized test scoring facility. Still, the couple had their problems. Hammerspace elaborates, "She didn't stop slutting around so much as she just changed into a completely joyless bitch no one would want to [expletive] anyway. Can I say that? Are you allowed to print that?"

With his issues at home becoming more and more frustrating, Melvin used his position at the testing facility to vent. "You know those tests you take in grade school where you fill in the little bubbles with a number two pencil and ship them somewhere to have them graded? I worked at that place." Melvin was written up twice for misconduct on the job. "They caught me changing some kid's name to 'condom break' on his test results. He was just so dumb and I was so angry I had to do it. In a lot of ways, that was my first act of villainy. It wasn't quite super yet, though."

After a succession of similar occurrences, Melvin was fired from the testing facility. He was determined not to let Linda find out. He began spending his days at the local shopping mall under the guise of working. "I would hang around and play arcade games. I got really good at Street Fighter. And that was actually how I discovered my powers. I was in the arcade with some friends and we worked out this system where we were cheating the ski ball machine. We had a guy behind it and one of us would roll him the balls under the machine and he would drop them in the center hole. So we accumulated this crazy amount of prize tickets and we used them to buy 849 packs of Pokemon stickers. We got so many we didn't think we could carry them all. I just started sticking them in my pockets and that's how I figured it out."

Melvin's newfound superpowers led to a rash of small time crime. "When you have an entire alternate universe of storage space readily available on your person it's the easiest thing in the world to steal things," he explains. "I could walk into a hardware store and walk out with a lawnmower, a chainsaw and a propane grill in my duster any day of the week. I remember, in the middle of Circuit City, jamming a fifty inch flat screen in my pants right in front of the security guy and like ten other people. The cops searched me up and down and had to let me walk."

At home, Linda was becoming suspicious. The apartment had slowly accumulated several items which were obviously not affordable on a test scorer's hourly wages – items including the aforementioned television, a whole range of stereo equipment, DVD players, gold ingots and a growing collection of original Monets. "I'm a big fan of impressionism. You know Monet was the most consistent and prolific practitioner of the movement's philosophy of expressing one's perceptions before nature, especially as applied to plein-air landscape painting." (I later found this exact line, stated verbatim, at the beginning of the Wikipedia entry for Monet. It was taken from *Monet in the 20th Century* by John House.)

In an attempt to distract Linda from his sudden and mysterious accumulation of wealth, Melvin proposed to her in a lavish New York restaurant with a full carat ring he purchased from Tiffany's & Co. Despite a long history protesting the global diamond trade, Linda accepted. The marriage was short lived. "If she was cranky before that she turned into a full on, frothing at the mouth, wretched velociraptor after we got married. It lasted about a year."

Thanks to her particularly shrewd attorney, Dick

SUPERVILLAINOUS!

Morgan, Linda secured an unusually high alimony payment in the divorce. Looking back, Hammerspace had this to say: "I know now that you don't get married to fix things. Getting married just makes things harder if it does anything at all. The divorce was awful. What a mess. And Dick Morgan is an asshole. I don't care what people say about him," he pauses and then adds "I guess the up side was that afterwards I had more time to dedicate to my career."

CHAPTER FIVE

After the super battle I'm slightly shaken, but not stirred. I call Larry from a payphone and excitedly tell him there's far more here than a three page magazine article. This is at least a book. For a moment I feel like Truman Capote when he first set foot in Holcomb, Kansas.

I walk down the street after hanging up on the perplexed and slightly annoyed Larry, who adamantly insists I cut this down to whatever Trigger wants. I'm in a fugue. I don't know how to find Hammerspace now. He effectively lost me when he vanished into that puff of smoke a few chapters ago.

I'm a few blocks from the payphone when I spot the flashing lights of police cars and fire trucks. I keep walking toward the disturbance until my way is blocked by police officers and a line of crime scene tape. On the other side of the police perimeter is a furiously burning gasoline tanker which firefighters scramble to spray with extinguishers. A way off from the tanker I see two paramedics hoisting the invisible remains of Force Field Girl into an ambulance. Apparently she ran from the battle with Hammerspace and was hit by a car (because she was invisible), which then lost control and careened into the parked gasoline tanker, causing it to explode. I can't help wondering about causality after this. If Foursight had never said anything, perhaps she wouldn't have run. But then maybe Hammerspace's grenade would have blown her apart. What exactly did Foursight see? Was it exactly this? Was this the only possibility? Was it like watching a television or was it much more complicated than seeing one scene at a time in the order that they go down? Maybe he sees all possible futures simultaneously, but somehow he can pick the one that will actually occur because of what he knows about the present. This awes me for a moment before I decide Foursight just isn't that smart, and I shake the notion.

I return to my hotel room and flip the TV on just for the noise to keep me company. I lie down and stare at the ceiling as I dial Hammerspace's cell phone number hopelessly. I'm shocked when he actually picks up. I stumble on my words at first, but it's surprisingly easy to convince him to meet up again.

It's three in the afternoon when Hammerspace picks me up from the sidewalk in front of the hotel in a green Honda Accord complete with rust holes. I assume this is a cover, because driving around in some sort of super car would draw too much attention. I immediately ask him about the disappearing act, and he assures me it isn't any sort of super power, only a slight of hand trick that anyone can do. He won't tell me exactly how it works, though.

We drive back to Hammerspace's building. I'm pretty excited to see the inside of a supervillain's lair, but what awaits on the other side of the door is shockingly normal. Hammerspace lives in a studio apartment on the third floor of a building that smells alarmingly of cat urine. He explains that this is because of the cat lady on the floor below him. I ask him how many of the animals she has and he says "none, but she keeps her litter box in the stairwell."

The inside of the villain's hive is cluttered with peculiar items. He has a chemistry set complete with boiling beakers atop bunsen burners and enormous lengths of twisty wires connecting them all to a large Tesla coil. There is a rifle-like device which is clearly labeled 'brain scrambler'. A man-sized robot spider sits deactivated behind his couch. A baseball diamond is displayed prominently inside a glass case near the entryway. A discarded sock hangs over the edge of the display case. Hammerspace passes all of this to sit down in a dilapidated reclining chair in front of the television. He kicks off his boots and puts up the foot rest. He reaches down and plucks an open bag of pork grinds from the floor next to the chair. He offers me some, but I decline. They give me heartburn.

Hammerspace seems more and more annoyed as I inquire excitedly about his death rays and robospiders. "You act like you've never seen a brainwashing machine before," he eventually interrupts. "It's not that big a deal. They don't even come in handy very often. Maybe when the death ray runs dry. You haven't seen a death ray either? They're all over the place."

I get him to talk more about the global super weapons black market. "There are a couple of evil super scientists out there that build this stuff and pretty much sell to the highest bidder. Some of it comes from space aliens too, but don't write that in your article. It pisses off the fundamentalist Christians. Super scientists? They're like scientists but they do super science. Super science is like regular science, but way ahead. That's where all the lasers and stuff come from. It's all powered by radioactive waves. You can get radiation to do just about anything."

Hammerspace sees something on the television that catches his eye and he reaches over to his coffee table for a tiny black spiral notepad. He jots something down and then explains. "This is where I write down all of my evil schemes. I like to write things out and let them sit for a little while before I really put anything in motion. Sometimes you come back to it later and realize it's just stupid. Like one time I came up with a plan to make kinoki pads that suck people's souls out of their feet. I had been drinking, but still. I come up with so many ideas. The mind of an evil genius is always rattling away. The gears never stop turning. Like this here, I just saw that kid from The Sixth Sense on TV and that made me think of this thing where you would pay it backward."

Pay it backward?

"Yeah. Basically, I'll go out and perform three evil deeds on complete strangers and I'll tell them to perform three evil deeds on three strangers. So it will spread like a chain letter until everybody on the planet is evil."

And that accomplishes…?

"Well, that's the part I haven't ironed out yet, but that's why I write these things down and come back to them. It's good to look at things from a fresh perspective so you can really weed out the bad ones."

Ever wonder what kinds of things an evil mastermind watches on TV? He lists his favorites for me as he surfs channels. "The Sopranos, American Idol, Family Matters reruns, COPS – I love COPS. I love watching degenerates get their asses beat."

Degenerates?

"Oh yeah, you know. Crack hos, junkies, trailer trash, to some extent drug dealers, just scumbags in general."

I should probably be a little afraid to ask the next question, but my reputation for having no tact and no fear must be upheld, so I do it. I ask him what divides him from those kinds of people.

His masked face twists into an appalled contortion I can't replicate in any literary way. "Are you joking? I'm nothing like those people. I mean, I suppose I understand where the average Joe might lump us all together as criminals, but that's like saying Hitler and Pam Anderson are the same because they're vegetarians. It just doesn't work. What I do I do with class. Those people are animals. They're little more than chimps given an orgasm button in some sort of lab experiment. They just push it and push it until they waste away and die. They have no self control, no ability to plan ahead, no greater thought processes, and no idea what they're doing. But I know exactly what I'm doing. I have plans and ambition. If I had to pick one special thing that separates us that would be it, the ambition. Real people have it. Dirt bags don't."

This ties into another interesting aspect of Hammerspace, which has become even more evident as he sits here watching TV - his total shift in diction when addressing superheroes as opposed to the way he speaks to me during everyday encounters. "Yeah. That's a big part of it. If I'm robbing a bank and the Scarlet Avenger lands in front of me and I say 'I ain't do nothin', bitch' that's how a common hood rat talks. I want the Scarlet Avenger to know that I'm a vastly superior threat. So I might say something like 'Well, well, well, Scarlet Avenger, we meet again. Shall we dance the dance where you DIE!' That sounds very chill. I'm letting her know I'm an educated and reasonable gentleman, but that I want to kill her."

So if this were Dungeons and Dragons you would be lawful evil?

"I have no idea what that means. I'm not a nerd-" is all he manages to say before he sees something that makes him leap out of his seat. "Holy shit!"

CHAPTER SIX

Hammerspace paces back and forth as he excitedly shouts into a cell phone at someone called Fumigator. The side of the conversation I can hear is
disappointingly vague. I'm only able to pick up a few
blurry details that weren't reported already on television, but this much is certain: El Malo Grande is
dead.

El Malo Grande, the hulking and terrifying figure
at the head of the Global Crime League, was killed
this afternoon in an altercation with unknown assail-
ants at his volcano fortress on Tibia Island in the
Central Pacific (approximately forty kilometers
southwest of Skull Island). Eventually Hammerspace
hangs up the phone and I'm able to get his inside perspective on what happened.

"Somebody freaking whacked him while he was
tanning by his pool. They dropped right into his fortress and whacked him! Fumigator thinks it was
██████████. He heard Malo killed a few of them be-

fore they got him."

Hammerspace begins a long explanation (at my request) as he mixes tea in his kitchen. "The GCL is the ultimate brotherhood of evil-doers. There are usually eight or ten of them and different guys are in or out at different times, but they're the biggest, baddest, most famous villains out there, real legends – guys like Doom Machine and Mr. Meltdown, household names. Everybody wants an invite to the GCL. They run the show in the world of supervillainy. They're kind of like CAA or The William Morris Agency in that way, only not quite as vicious."

For the record, the current GCL line up consists of: Mr. Meltdown, with his ability to turn anything he looks at to mush, Principal Uncertainty, the ex-high school administrator who can be in two places at once and walk through walls, Doom Machine, an alien cyborg with a massive complement of built-in destructive devices, Dark Pope, the infallible supreme pontiff of the church of atheism, The Schrodinger, who is immortal as long as no one is looking at him, Ghettoblaster, able to project massive explosions by beatboxing, Osama Bin Laden, and, until today, El Malo Grande, the invincible and super strong Latino leader of the group.

"The ███████, and this is the stuff you won't read in the paper, is a super secret organization that conducts operations all over the globe. They do some policing of the super beings occasionally."

So they're kind of like Interpol, but for supervillains?

"Are they like Interpol? If Interpol will make you watch them murder your infant to get information about security threats and laugh at you when you bring up the Geneva convention then yeah, they're like Interpol."

So they're not good guys?

"No. Superheroes are good guys. The police man that helps you find your mommy when you're lost is a good guy. ███████ are definitely bad guys. Well, I guess they're good guys when they fight us because we're the bad guys, but they play both sides of the fence too. And these are the scariest guys out there. They have kill teams that do nothing but murder people and leave no trace they were ever there. The worst of them is ████████████."

And they work for?

"Nobody knows. Well, I mean obviously they know, but – it's an expression. You know what I mean. I think they're Americans or maybe NATO or something because they have a lot of fancy gear. You know those stories you hear about black unmarked helicopters buzzing cattle mutilations and stuff? That's them. Skullface told me he thinks they work for the lizard people, but he smokes a ton of weed and sometimes paranoia is an issue for him."

The lizard people?

"There aren't really lizard people. Well, unless you count Fumigator. Is an alligator a lizard? I'm not sure."

An alligator is a reptile, and what Hammerspace says about the ████████ is completely uncorroborated by any reputable sources, although some details are occasionally backed by supermarket tabloids. News rags like that are full of reports of black, unmarked helicopters, secret societies and government cover-ups, and they also run headlines claiming the president is having an affair with a space alien. Although I've heard the name ███████ thrown around here and there during my research, I'm far from convinced there is actually such a group. The evidence is sketchy at best. Reports are nearly all second or third hand, and even The Toxic Shocker, whom Hammerspace met in person and claimed to have worked for the group, has a reputation for making ridiculous claims to pump up his social stature. There's no good reason to see this as anything more than an urban legend imagined by bewildered super people to explain that which they have no control over.

I'm deeply fascinated that a supervillain would put stock in a myth like this. Normal people fear the boogeyman (real or imaginary). Peculiar is the idea that the boogeyman checks under his bed for something even scarier before he goes to sleep.

"Anyway, this is huge. With El Malo Grande dead there's going to be a major shake up. The GCL will be out for blood after this, and lots of guys will be pulling off the most ridiculous stuff they can come up with trying to score creds to impress them so they can get a spot on the team. All hell could break loose pretty fast."

Getting street cred in the world of supervillainy is no easy task. Anybody can hold up a bank or tie a pretty girl to some railroad tracks, especially if they have decent super powers. The GCL doesn't bother talking to villains unless they've become a household name by themselves. Usually villains have to trigger an event that has some sort of global implications to gain that sort of status. Doom Machine got his invite after he broke the Scarlet Avenger's spine and left her a paraplegic (she was healed by undisclosed means after a year on the sidelines). The Schrodinger summoned a planet eating monster from another dimension into the middle of New York City to get invited (superheroes eventually teleported it to Soviet Russia, where it was eaten by the planet). Osama Bin Laden... Well, you already know what he did to join the team.

"Every guy's dream is to do some shit like that and end up getting a major crossover. Crossover is a business term. It's when a bunch of superheroes have to team up to defeat you. The more the better. Schrodinger pulled that off with the monster thing. Scarlet Avenger got brainwashed by Demento. That was huge. He got killed in that though. The biggest was El Malo Grande. It was after he was on the team already. He did that thing where he stole Amazing Man's powers and tried to launch a nuke into the Earth's core. He took on General Welfare, The Crusaders, Power Team and The Magician by himself. That's what legends are made of."

But now the legend is dead, leaving a massive void that seems likely to be filled by terrifying violence and also a plethora of nagging questions. Who did this (if not the folkloric culprits of Hammerspace's imagination)? And how exactly does one kill an invincible man? "I wish I knew," Hammerspace says. "Of course most invincible guys aren't actually invincible per se. They're just ridiculously durable. It's not always easy to tell the difference, but believe me, just because a guy can take a wrecking ball in the face and walk away doesn't mean he can swim in molten lava or eat a dirty bomb for breakfast. It's all different. Now your truly invincible guys, there isn't much to be done with them except remove them from play somehow. You can freeze them or encase them in bronze or something. Stasis fields are a possibility, but they cost a damn fortune. I tried to get one to use on General Welfare. You ever walk into a bank and tell a loan officer you need thirty million dollars to entrap a superhero within a boundary of infinite rigidity and time suspension? There's no FHA for evil conquerors. You're on your own in this business."

****

Hammerspace watches *Pride and Prejudice* on the television as I bring back a sandwich from the deli around the block. The sight throws me at first and he has to explain. "Hollywood is too much like work for me. You know I see explosions and guys throwing buildings and flying people every day on the job. When I come home I want to relax with something that takes the edge off. I'm a big fan of Merchant Ivory productions and I have a lot of nineties sitcom boxed sets. I love *Family Matters. Frasier* is great too. Besides, movies get so much stuff wrong. It's annoying. I mean, how many times do you see a movie where the main character is a writer and it just drives you crazy pointing out all the things they got wrong?"

He makes a point. In the movies writers are often rich, good looking and charismatic. In reality we have difficulty paying the bills and spend most of our lives alone with a word processor. I won't complain about the good looking part. At least in my case, they got that right.

"It's inescapable. The worst is the henchmen. Nobody really has henchmen. I guess a few of the really rich guys do, but I've never had a henchman. I've never even met a henchman. Can you see that classified ad? 'Wanted: Individuals to commit crimes in matching costumes for low pay. Will be murdered after too many failures.' Who's going to take that job? And what do they put on their tax return?"

He goes on about henchmen for a while before moving to the subject of villainous plans. "They don't always think these things through in fictional portrayals. Bad guys are always trying to destroy the world in comic books. That doesn't make sense. We have to live here too. Why would we do that?"

On superheroes. "There's no way, super powers or not, that anyone can stumble on as many crimes in progress as the superheroes in comics. It's like every time they walk down the street something happens. 'Oh look, the bank is getting robbed. I better intervene.' That doesn't happen. One of the main reasons I use my super powers for evil is that I get to stir up interesting situations instead of waiting around for them to happen. Superheroes aren't allowed to do that. It has to be incredibly boring."

On costumes. "How the hell do people not recognize them? Superman? All he does is take off his glasses. It's absurd! Nobody in this business is getting by with anything less than two thirds of their face covered. Most do just the uncovered mouth thing like I do, but a lot of guys go full ski mask with just the eyes uncovered. I can think of one or two women that tried that opera mask look, and it's sort of sexy, but it's how you end up with large super powered rapists waiting at your apartment when you get home. That's what happened to Fire Dancer." Indeed, and you can read about it in her book, *Getting By: Life As a Sexual Assault Survivor.*

On the few realistic fictional heroes. "There aren't any I can think of that are spot on. The worst are usually the ones normal people find the most plausible, like Watchmen. They don't even have super powers. Nobody makes it in this business without super powers. Batman could never happen. It's ridiculous. Do you have any idea what it's like to fight people who can pick up a fire truck and throw it at you? I have an infinite supply of munitions on me and it's still way too hard. That guy has a utility belt and he knows karate. What the hell is that? And I'm not saying nobody has ever tried it. I know they have. None of them last very long."

CHAPTER SEVEN

"What I really need," says Hammerspace as he jogs along in a track suit and headband (over his mask) "is to really lay the smack down on General Welfare."

Keeping pace with us is Fumigator, a seven foot tall monster of a man wearing a tank of poison gas and an elaborate alligator mask complete with a muzzle and teeth. It covers his face completely and his voice comes through as a muffled echo. He replies, "Yeah. That guy is an asshole."

I asked Fumigator earlier about the gator theme and the poison. He filled me in. "I went with the gator theme because I went to the University of Florida. That's actually where I had the accident that left me completely immune to all types of poison gas, hence the fumes - fumigator. The mask is actually made from a real alligator head. A friend of mine is a taxidermist. I can give you his card if you want. It has a lot of scare factor, and that's something you want, but it's a pain if I get an itch or a runny nose or something."

One of the most important parts of the villain's lifestyle is regular exercise. In order to do battle with the likes of superpowered do gooders, supervillains need to stay in shape. Cardio is a must and weight training is also pretty typical. That's why Hammerspace and Fumigator go on a daily 5k run. They stick together just to be safe in the event that they might run into a superhero. Although the possibility is slim, this is still a good idea. One of the worst super fights in history occurred in August 1991 when Knight Watch ran into Brute Suit in New York's central park whilst walking their dogs. The two began a scuffle over Brute Suit's alleged neglect to pick up his dog's leavings, which escalated into an all out battle to the death. Ultimately, a large area of the park was left a desolate, crater-covered wasteland. Both Knight Watch and Brute Suit were killed by a National Guard armored division. Ever since, costumed super characters have been more careful about these things, and a buddy system is never a bad plan.

Fumigator met Hammerspace during a routine bank heist in 2006. "I walked into the bank with my poison gun ready to go and I yell everybody down, but then I realize they're already on the floor," Fumigator recalls. "That's when I walk back to the vault and see this dickhead cramming safety deposit boxes, I mean the whole boxes, into his coat. He wasn't even opening them."

"I open them with a cutting torch back at my apartment," Hammerspace interjects.

"I didn't know that then. So I was just confused,

you know? There's this guy doing my job and we end up in sort of a stand off for a minute. But then in walks... What was his name?" He laughs as Hammerspace jogs his memory. "That's right! The Peacekeeper! What a costard. His power was that nobody could commit acts of violence in his presence – including him. So Hammerspace just kept taking stuff. What was he going to do? We both laughed so hard. I think we literally laughed him out of the business. I remember the security guard standing there yelling at him to do something."

Hammerspace continues to bounce ideas off of Fumigator. "Do you think he gets his powers from the sun? I could find a way to block it out."

Fumigator seems unreceptive to this idea. "He kicked the crap out of Doom Machine at night once. I saw it."

"Maybe he stores energy during the day," Hammerspace counters.

Fumigator shakes his head. "Nah."

"See, invulnerable heroes usually have some kind of Achilles heel, you know, like... uh... That guy (Achilles)" Fumigator tells me. "If we can figure out General Welfare's secret weakness we can take advantage. So far we've tried poison gas, well, obviously (he points to his gas tank), death rays, ultra mega death rays, radioactive minerals. Hammerspace dropped an anvil on him from a building. Other guys have tried acid, magic spells, bombs, undersea pressure, aphorbic bombs - you name it. It's been done. He takes a licking."

"Didn't Terrortron nuke him once?" Hammerspace adds.

"Yeah, during the Uzbekistan thing. That was ugly."

I can't help but picture General Welfare taking an ICBM the size of a building square in his puffed out chest, smiling the whole time. The blast incinerates his costume in milliseconds but he remains, walking from the charred crater of scorched earth stark naked, his smug expression never changing. What does a person think as the air catches fire around them and everything that was ceases to be? Is it absolute terror, or is it as mundane as a drive to work? As his hair was burning off in ten million degree temperatures was he wondering what he would do for lunch? Or is his hair invincible too?

"What about the stasis field bomb idea? What happened with that?" Fumigator asks.

Hammerspace rolls his eyes. "I can't show a two year work history and unless you get me into Fort Knox to load my coat with gold bricks, we don't have the funds."

It is at this point in their conversation that I interrupt to ask a question I suspect I will regret later (and I do, although not to the extent that some would have you believe). I ask Hammerspace why he can't simply break into the place where they keep the stasis generators and toss one into his jacket.

He laughs. "They're too big to fit in my jacket. I would need somebody to forklift it off the ground and then I still couldn't conceal it anywhere."

Fumigator interjects. "Isn't the whole point of your super power that you don't have to conceal anything?"

"Well, sort of. I have to be able to hide things initially but then they just sort of… poof. They're gone."

"Don't you wonder about that? Where does all that stuff go?"

"To the Hammerspace. That's why I'm Hammerspace. I mean, I thought that was established."

"Yeah, but what is it exactly? Is it like another dimension? What's it like in there?"

"I don't know. I've never been in there. I don't think that's even possible. That's like a snake eating its own tail or something."

"Have you ever thrown anything alive in there?"

An hour later we're in a pet shop off the turnpike somewhere. Hammerspace is buying a big bunny rabbit, which Fumigator picked out because he thinks the idea of making a rabbit disappear is more hilarious than any other animal we could have chosen. He buys a small dog leash to go with it.

We don't even leave the pet store to conduct the first experiment. Hammerspace puts the leash on the animal. I make a joke about the first bunny rabbit shot into Hammerspace. Neither of them thinks it's funny. I've never been funny.

Fumigator picks up the rabbit, which is a fat rabbit. It doesn't move around a lot. He pulls the rabbit around on the leash for a while to make sure it can't get loose. We're getting a ton of stares from people in the pet shop now. A lady with a Siamese cat asks me if we're doing some kind of TV show and for the first time I wonder if people around us see figures of legendary greatness or if they ogle simply because a grown man in an alligator costume is walking a rabbit on a dog leash. Hammerspace points this out to Fumigator and they get on with the experiment before we gather any more unwanted attention.

Hammerspace holds his trench coat open and Fumigator tosses the rabbit at him. He closes the jacket and the bunny is gone. Its leash dangles from the folds of Hammerspace's jacket. Fumigator stares strangely at this, and even Hammerspace seems somewhat perplexed. "I've never had anything alive go in there, and I've never had any sort of lifeline dangling out either. So this is a first for a couple things. It's kind of weird because you can actually make out where this place ends and the nowhere be- gins. I'm gonna be pissed if that thing gets lost in there. Who knows what it could get into. The last thing I need is a rabbit running around eating up my store of Nutrigrain bars. What if it dies? Everything I pull out of there is going to smell terrible."

Fumigator hangs on to the leash for a few minutes to see if the rabbit tugs at all. We get nothing. He shrugs. Hammerspace reaches into the coat and pulls out the rabbit. Fumigator is somewhat im- pressed, but he says that in order to be certain we need to send the rabbit in without the leash to see if Hammerspace can still retrieve it. We do. Ham- merspace pulls it back out a moment later with no difficulty.We all immediately know the next step, al- though it is Fumigator who brings it up first.

"I've got to go in." He says.

Hammerspace is more reluctant. "I don't know. I think that's kind of gay."

"What?"

"Jumping into another guy's hammerspace. It's just kind of gay, that's all."

"Whatever, Richard Gere. You put a rabbit in

there already. By that logic you just committed bestiality."

A fifteen minute argument then ensues, which I won't reproduce here because it is completely pointless and somewhat homophobic. I'm not saying I stand by the gay agenda, only that I need this book to appeal to as many readers as possible.

Finally, Hammerspace and Fumigator turn to me and demand I settle the argument. I tell them I'd personally like to know what's in there, and frankly, I can't believe no one has thought of this before.

Hammerspace caves after Fumigator bothers him a little bit longer and they decide to give it a test run, but Hammerspace still insists that we find a female person for this experiment. Being a supervillain, Fumigator concedes that it does make more sense to toss a civilian into the Hammerspace before he risks his own life. The two of them settle on a cashier named Debbie whom Fumigator gasses with some sort of poison. As she wobbles and topples he scoops her off her feet and tosses her unconscious body into Hammerspace's jacket.

Bystanders begin screaming and running when they see this. We run down the street and wait for ten minutes or so in an alley, during which time Hammerspace notes aloud that he's never had anyone throw anything into the hammerspace before. He tells me this has given him a really wicked idea, but he won't elaborate any more on the subject.

Once the coast is clear and the guys have determined that no superheroes are coming to the rescue, Hammerspace pulls a hysterical pet store clerk from the confines of his infinite storage space. I try to ask her what it was like in there, but she runs away.

It is Fumigator who points out the most important thing we have learned from this experiment. "Once something goes in there, it can't leave until Hammerspace pulls it out.

CHAPTER EIGHT

It's Friday afternoon and I'm at the Stanley Lloyd Kaufman Middle school in Sunman, Indiana, a god-forsaken place where there is no cell phone reception for miles, winningest is considered a proper word, and the value of a man is the number of inches his lift kit adds to his pick-up.

I'm here officially to cover a Hugs not Drugs lecture by Jose Canyousee, General Welfare's teenage sidekick. I'm here unofficially because supervillains hinted that something might be going down. I'm sitting in a folding chair in the back row and I'm wearing a business casual ensemble so I don't stand out. I have a hefty camera so I look like a press photographer and I used an old press pass to get in (you wouldn't believe the security in public schools these days). I've also got a flak jacket under my clothes that I picked up at the police uniform supply store. The damn thing cost a fortune and I honestly don't think it will provide much protection if death rays and laser beams start zapping around the room, but I might as well do what I can.

It's two o'clock by the time the auditorium is full and kids between the ages of eleven and fifteen (I figure there must be a few flunkies) sit talking to their friends and appearing generally unexcited about the coming performance. A few teachers have to snap their fingers and shoosh the rowdier students when the lights go down. The show opens with an over-the-hill volunteer band and some rejected Disney World backup dancers doing a lame song about the dangers of drug use. I spot more than one Bob Marley shirt in the crowd of kids during this time.

At the end of the musical number Jose comes out amidst a howling high note introduction from the dance crew and starts telling the kids about the dangers of drug use. He's wearing his trademark spandex American flag costume with cowboy chaps. I think his intentions are good, but this doesn't seem to be a good way to reach these kids. Looking around the room I notice quite a few of them are more interested in their cell phones than what is happening on stage. That all changes in seconds.

An explosion rocks the building as the rear auditorium doors are blasted off their hinges. Hammerspace steps into the building pointing the Mallet of Malice at Jose across the crowded room. He issues a threat in his thunderous villain voice. "Jose, can you see your demise at my hands!"

Remarkably, the entire crowd is unshaken. Everyone is paying attention now, but no one seems upset. It takes a moment for me to realize they all think this is part of the show. I, knowing this not to be the case, am ironically more unsettled than everyone else.

"The Trenchcoat!" shouts Jose from the stage.

"It's Hammerspace, dick!" reprimands the villain."

"I've already sent a distress call to General Welfare, Trenchcoat. Your days as a criminal mastermind are numbered!"

"Even at his fastest, General Welfare can't get here in time to stop me from killing you!"

"Whoa! The k word? In front of the kids? That's totally not cool."

"What?"

"You're supposed to say destroy or vanquish or annihilate or something. Nobody says the k word. It's just unprofessional."

I'm caught off guard and I can see that Hammerspace is too. Jose has obviously been out of the game for a while. That or he's been in it for way too long.

"And even if you capture me and put me in your fastest acting death trap, the General will have time to get here and save me, so do your best, Trenchcoat!" he continues.

Hammerspace pulls a shotgun out of his jacket and shoots Jose in the guts. In truly diabolical fashion, he does this over the heads of several rows of students, who I'm fairly certain are able to feel the buckshot whizzing by their hair. He approaches the stage calmly as Jose attempts to crawl away.

"A gun! Guns are for cowards and losers-" he utters before Hammerspace finishes him off with another barrel full of buckshot.

"Oh, but I've won here," Hammerspace says,

turning to face the audience. "Go children! Run! Flee! Tell everyone what you have seen here today! Tell them so they may never forget the name of Hammerspace!" With that, he launches into a classic evil cackle that reverberates through the room. The boom mic picks it up and it echoes even more loudly. It reaches a deafening level as the children and the school faculty run panic stricken from the auditorium. I take cover behind some bleachers and continue to watch Hammerspace.

Once the room is empty, except for the two of us (and Jose's cadaver), I ask Hammerspace exactly what he's attempting here. "Killing the sidekick is a big move for any supervillain. If you want to establish yourself as the number one archnemesis, you have to kill someone really close to the hero," he answers. "That's why I tried to kill Welfare's woman a few weeks ago, but it turned out she was just some girl he went on one date with so I gave up on that." He has a point. After all, where would Green Goblin or Joker be had they not murdered Gwen Stacy and Jason Todd? As much as Hammerspace claims to dislike comic book characters, he draws a lot of his ideas from them.

Moments later, Hammerspace is gone, having discarded his costume and walked out of the building appearing like any normal schmoe. The usefulness of an alter ego hadn't quite demonstrated itself to me until now. As a normal guy, I tend to focus on the super side of everything. Super beings are very much the opposite. For them, the every day alter ego seems to be the more exciting. And it makes sense. After all, being super is their job, and which would you rather be? Yourself or yourself at work?

The secret identity, in fact, is arguably stronger than the super identity. It is easily more dangerous, because you don't see it coming. You never see it coming.

And so I'm still in the auditorium hours later interviewing police when General Welfare crashes through the concrete wall nearby and storms up to the stage. A few cops look like they might want to restrain him, and they almost begin to, but then their better judgment impedes them and they just stop what they're doing and stare helplessly. He leaps up on to the stage and cradles Jose's crumpled body in his arms. He shrieks "Nooooooooooooooooooooooo-ooooooooooooooo!"

"YES!" Shouts Hammerspace as he drops from a catwalk above the stage. No one saw this coming. He's been here the whole time.

"You! I'll kill you!" screams General Welfare.

"Oh, please, Welfare. We all know you have a strict no killing policy."

The General picks up a nearby cop and takes his gun, throwing the cop aside. He points the gun at Hammerspace and fires wildly. Hammerspace pulls his trench coat open wide like a perverted old man in a Chuck E Cheese. The bullets are sucked into another dimension.

Hammerspace cackles madly. "A feeble attempt from a feeble hero!" he taunts. "Soon you will join your pathetic boy child in oblivion!"

Welfare doesn't say anything. He rushes Hammerspace like a stampede on the Serengeti. I dive behind a theater seat, afraid there might be a shockwave from the impact when Welfare hits him. Instead, there is nothing.

I stand up from behind the chair and see the bottoms of General Welfare's boots disappearing into Hammerspace's trench coat. Hammerspace turns to face the small army of police surrounding him. Some of them pull guns but he shouts them down.

"Fire at me and you risk hitting your precious hero!" he says. No one shoots, even though this is entirely illogical. General Welfare is completely invincible. He takes missiles in the face like gnats hitting a windshield. I doubt bullets would offend him.

The police are powerless to stop him, and so Hammerspace simply walks out of the building and vanishes.

CHAPTER NINE

I'm sitting in the Mayor's office in New York. Well, it used to be the mayor's office. Now it belongs to Hammerspace. He lounges in a big leather chair with his feet on a desk that still harbors Mayor Bloomberg's metal name tag.

"Mayor Hammerspace just doesn't sound threatening enough. Mayor Hammerspace is a guy who invests in low risk mutual funds and walks to the other side of the street when he sees a black guy coming. It doesn't say ruthless dictator who holds the city within his iron grasp. That's what I am. This is my iron gauntlet of pain" he says as he holds up his right fist to demonstrate for me. He has been pondering this bizarre title situation since he took over the Mayor's office two days ago, in a coup that was carried out so easily the former city hall administration should be ashamed.

It went down like this: In the middle of a press conference in which the Mayor was all too happy to discuss General Welfare's disappearance rather than the specifics of the social equality legislation he was supporting, Hammerspace smashed in the doors to the press room with the Mallet of Malice and entered. The police were unable to stop him, largely because he had a nuclear explosive which he threatened to detonate if they tried anything, and he simply pushed the Mayor away from the podium and declared himself the new ruler of New York.

"I got the bomb from soviet defectors a few years ago. Where else do you get a nuclear bomb?" he answers when I ask him how he got his hands on the weapon.

Immediately after kicking the mayor off stage Hammerspace began making new laws and regulations right there at the podium. "For my first act as ruler of this city, I declare that every resident shall be taxed on forty percent of their income! If you do not pay your taxes you will be executed. In fact, all crimes committed in the city will now be punishable by death! Fear me, city of New York! Fear the asphyxiating grasp of despotism that is my rule!"

And so Hammerspace is still lying back in his chair when Fumigator walks into the office with surprising news. "They love you out there" he says. Hammerspace is taken aback, and frankly so am I.

"What?" he says, sitting up in his chair.

"Yeah. They're partying in the streets."

"Why? I burden them with the shackles of oppression and obscene taxes!"

"Well, no. Not really. You actually lowered the taxes. They were paying like sixty percent before."

I knew this before. But I didn't have the heart to

tell him. He seemed so excited about his despotism.

"What about the mandatory death penalty for all crimes? That has to have them pissing themselves."

"They're okay with it. The city had kind of a crime problem before so, you know. They're already talking about turning the prison into a conservatory or something."

"I really need to kick it in gear with the evilness here. What about something with abortion? People hate abortion. What about forced abortion of minorities?"

"That's pretty harsh, Mel."

"That's the point."

"But that will really piss people off. What if they revolt or something?"

"We'll confiscate all the guns first."

"I think New York already has a gun ban."

"Does anyone else see the irony here?"

Seconds later, a crimson colored glove shatters through the wall, only a few feet from the door, and into the room steps the famed and elusive Scarlet Avenger. Even the few existing photographs of her could not have possibly prepared me for this. In person, the Scarlet Avenger burns with an aura of intensity hotter than the sun. The movement of her hips as she walks is like the violent thrashing of an ocean vessel in a tropical storm. Her bouncing red hair shimmers like diamonds in an inferno. Her long slender legs lift the feet of a princess and each time they crash back down the earth quakes beneath them. Her perfect figure is the envious rage of every supermodel enveloped in crimson shrink-wrap. Briefly she turns her head and I dare to look in her eyes for a fraction of a fraction of a second before the most furious intimidation I have ever known threatens to tear my soul apart.

Fumigator sums this all up with "Dude." Then Scarlet Avenger choke slams him through the floor. Yes. All the way through the floor. I could never have come up with that. She's creative too.

Hammerspace already has the suitcase nuke in his hand and he's brandishing it for her to see. "Stand back, Scarlet whore. Even you can't survive a nuclear-" Then she kicks him in the nuts and takes the suitcase away.

She turns to me with a glare of focused rage and for the first time I hear her voice. She says "who the hell are you?" with a thick English accent that allows her to sound pissed off and yet still more refined than the classiest debutante. The Scarlet Avenger is English? There are British superheroes? Instead of answering her I'm thrown by this notion for a moment. Then I realize how ignorant it is. She has to repeat herself. This makes her a little less refined.

I tell her I'm an embedded journalist reporting on supervillains for Trigger magazine. She drops her guard, confused and says "Well, that's just ace then. I'm glad rock and roll magazines are still busy promoting positive role models." I think she's being sarcastic. A moment ago I couldn't look at her, but now it's hard not to.

She punches into the suitcase nuke and rips out a big chunk of colored wires as she approaches my chair. She drops the clump of wires to the ground and with her free hand reaches into her cleavage to fish around for something. "You know, I'm promoting my new album," she says as she pulls a red business card from her costume, which upon closer inspection, is some sort of ultra glossy rubber. "I don't usually do interviews, but maybe that can change."

Across the room, unbeknownst to her, Hammerspace peels himself up from the floor and draws an anti-tank weapon from his jacket. He takes only a second to aim as I curiously examine the Scarlet Avenger's business card. I note that the card lists contact information for an agency that represents her, but not her own info.

Hammerspace pulls the trigger and his bazooka emits a deafening ka-pow which echoes throughout the building and hurts my ears. All of the windows in the room shatter as the Scarlet Avenger catches the shell in her hand with all the difficulty of a major league infielder in a softball game. She puts a hand on her hip and smiles back to him. "That was quite a googly," she says as she tosses the impacted artillery round over her shoulder. "Now tell me what you've done with General Welfare and I might let you live."

Hammerspace cackles loudly. "Everyone knows you have a strict no-kill policy, Scarlet Harlot. I'll see your bet and raise you dead bystanders." With that he smiles and tosses a plastic explosive out a nearby window.

In a blur, Scarlet Avenger flies out the window in a race to catch the bomb before it lands in the street. Hammerspace turns to me and shouts as he runs from the room. "We have to get out of here! That bought us like ten seconds if we're lucky!"

I chase him down the hallway toward the stairwell. As we're running by the elevator he pushes the button to call it, but he keeps running. He shouts back "Elevators are a terrible escape route, but if you push the button sometimes you can trick a superhero into thinking you're in there." Sure enough, we hear Scarlet Avenger peeling the steel elevator doors open as we're running down the stairs into the basement.

We find Fumigator in the basement and Hammerspace drags him to his feet. Hammerspace yells at him. "We have to go! She's right behind us!"

CHAPTER TEN

I'm chasing Hammerspace and Fumigator through an alleyway outside New York City Hall. We've just been attacked by the Scarlet Avenger, one of the most recognized superheroes in the world, despite her well documented aversion to all forms of media. I haven't seen any sign of destruction outside the building and I'm beginning to wonder how she stopped that bomb Hammerspace threw out the window from demolishing everything on the street level, when I hear an unusual wooshing sound.

Hammerspace yells "Move!" and he and Fumigator both dive for the pavement as a huge dumpster crashes to the ground narrowly missing them both. I look up to see Scarlet Avenger slowly levitating down to the ground with us, her arms crossed smugly. The woman is the hottest kind of ice. She never ever loses her cool.

"Maybe I can't kill you, Hammerspace, but I can hurt you so bad you won't want to live anymore," she says as Hammerspace and Fumigator regain their feet. "Now let General Welfare go or I'll start breaking parts of you."

Suddenly, the strangest thing I've ever seen happens right in front of me. Something explodes all over the back of Scarlet Avenger's head and puffs out into a cloud of brown dust that scatters little specs across her shoulders. She screams in agony and turns around.

Behind her stands a man in a fine grey suit with wonderfully combed hair and the longest eighteenth century style side burns I have ever seen. He holds a can of Hershey's cocoa powder in his perfectly groomed fingers. He is the Schrodinger.

Scarlet Avenger reels. She clearly is having difficulty staying on her feet. The Schrodinger speaks up. "Like most women, the Scarlet Avenger has a weakness for chocolate. However, hers is quite a bit more acute. Isn't that right, dear?"

"Eat shit, Schrodinger," she says.

The Schrodinger licks his knuckles and puts his fist in the can of cocoa powder. "I find that dark is preferable to milk, but the cocoa powder is most potent, especially when it's moistened for maximum stickiness." We all watch as the Schrodinger punches her in the face so hard even Hammerspace winces. I can hear the cracking of her nose. Somehow, she keeps standing. Wet, brown powder sticks to her face. "You see, as long as the powder adheres to her, she's completely powerless." He hits her again, this time so hard she spins around on the balls of her feet and faces us for a second before she drops to the pavement.

The Schrodinger dumps the rest of the cocoa on her crumpled form. He turns to the rest of us. "Come along now. As much as I enjoy battering that red headed slut, Power Team will be here momentarily and, sadly, we haven't the numbers to fight them."

The Schrodinger takes us to a black limousine which is waiting nearby and we jump in. The driver peels out and we're leaving the city in the dust.

Two hours later we're on the Schrodinger's private jet headed for some secret installation hidden somewhere out in the ocean I'm assuming, although I have no idea for certain. One thing is for sure, though. The Schrodinger travels in style. We're talking leather interior, sound system, a full bar – he spares no expense. I make a point to sit down with him during the flight.

"What can I say? My business is being bad and business is good. No really. You tend to amass a lot of wealth over so many centuries. I still have money in the stock exchange from the twenties. It really is true what they say about making your money work for you. I haven't worked since the depression."

How did you come to be unkillable?

"I don't know. I was just always that way. It can be a bit odd, considering most in this business developed abilities after an accident of some type or an encounter with magical beings or one of a dozen different common things, but I simply am what I am."

He tells me he knew Hammerspace would be in trouble once he heard about General Welfare's disappearance, and that the murderous trench coated bad guy has developed a following in the villain community over the last two days. "Since what happened to

Malo we've seen a lot of stunts pulled by upstart fire-brands — punks wanting attention mostly. But what Hammerspace did is very inspiring. Not many villains have defeated a superhero like that. I cannot think of the last time it happened. And the way he executed the sidekick was just refreshing. You don't see that kind of ruthlessness usually these days. He's certainly caught some important eyes, if you catch my meaning."

He has significantly worse things to say about the Scarlet Avenger. "I first found out about the chocolate trick when she tried to break up my plot to put mind control serum in the Los Angeles water supply. The treatment plant was right next door to a Nestle packing facility. Doom Machine was working for me as sort of a bodyguard at the time. He threw her into the building and she went crashing through the wall and into a bunch of supply crates and chocolate bars were all over her. She couldn't do anything. Once Doom Machine realized her powers didn't work he picked her up and snapped her in half. I was simply ecstatic. I made a tape recording of her screaming actually. I often listen to it when I... never mind." Yes. Please never mind.

Hammerspace kicks back in a seat at the rear of the plane. He seems surprised when I tell him what the Schrodinger had to say. "That's fine, but I don't want people thinking I just did it to impress the league. I did it because I'm evil. I'm like, way evil. Way more evil than you can possibly fathom. I'm ready to set a new precedent in the field, and I don't want people to say he's just doing it for attention, because I'm not."

One parachute jump later we're being picked up in a submarine that takes us deep beneath the sea to the Global Crime League's secret undersea dome. If you've never seen an undersea dome (I'm betting you haven't) it is really something to take a look at. The Schrodinger explains that under the ocean is truly the only place left to hide on planet Earth now that there are planes and satellites that can comb virtually all of the land space on the globe in a few short days.

Inside the dome we are greeted by a contingent of armed guards wearing shiny metal armor and carrying very expensive guns. These are the first actual henchmen I've met and I pick out one of the higher ranking members and ask some questions as they're leading us down a large corridor from the airlock. He identifies himself as Steve. "Yeah. I've been a henchman for eight years now. I used to sell cell phones, but once the market got saturated I had to find something else. I was hanging out with this guy, Ray, at the time and he was connected so he showed my resume around and got me in with Ghettoblaster. You really have to know somebody to break into this field."

And it isn't a cushy field to be in either. Danger and death lurk around every corner for the professional henchman. Assignments are often difficult and failure is not an option. "Doom Machine zapped Ray a few years ago after a run in with Fire Dancer. It was his own fault though. He had a whole squad of guys and she's not even class two."

Steve refers, of course, to the Defense Department's ranking system for superhuman threat assessment. For those of you who aren't familiar, it works like this: A class one superhuman has one relatively simple superpower. Fumigator and Fire Dancer (who shoots fire from her fingers) are class one superhumans. Class two superhumans have either multiple superhuman abilities or one superhuman ability with multiple applications. Hammerspace and Principal Uncertainty are class two superhumans. Class three superhumans have many super abilities with multiple applications and could represent a serious threat to national security by themselves. The Scarlet Avenger is a popular example of a class three superhuman. She could throw the White House into space if she wanted and an armored cavalry division could do nothing to stop her.

Now that Malo is dead and General Welfare is out of commission, the only other creature on the planet with that kind of power is Doom Machine and I find myself staring right at him.

CHAPTER ELEVEN

Doom Machine, the alien android from the planet Reaper Six Six Six in the Deathbringer Nebula, stands a full seven feet tall in his gold and green armored cyber body. His limbs are smooth plating sculpted to resemble a muscular humanoid figure and his eyes glow bright yellow. He stands at the center of a massive meeting chamber surrounded by the other members of the Global Crime League – Dark Pope, Ghettoblaster, Principal Uncertainty, and Mr. Meltdown. Osama Bin Laden was unable to make it to the meeting, as he is still in hiding.

"We must make the activation of the Chaos Engine our number one priority," Doom Machine barks in his echoing, metallic, robotic voice. The deadliest known supervillain in the world is truly frightening as he turns to acknowledge the Schrodinger. "What is this, Schrodinger? You've brought these insects to the secret meeting chamber?"

SUPERVILLAINOUS!

The Schrodinger stands smugly, and I'm surprised by his fearlessness, although I suppose it's difficult to be afraid of anything when you cannot die. "I see you're as impulsive as ever, Doom Machine. Remember who it was that brought you into the fold."

The Dark Pope, who sits in a huge obsidian chair, his face obscured by his massive pope hat, says something in Italian which is filtered to us by his interpreter. "Dark Pope say Doom Machine make a point. His unholiness want to know who these people are."

"The alligator man is Fumigator, master of poison gas, and to my left is Hammerspace," replies the Schrodinger. Someone gasps. Dark Pope's eyes widen. Doom Machine seems unsurprised, although it is difficult to gauge him as he seems to be in a persistent state of fury.

Dark Pope says something else in Italian. His translator speaks. "Dark Pope say wait, what about that other guy?"

"Yeah. Who dat be?" says Ghettoblaster, his cartoonish gold grill blinging as he speaks.

I step forward and start to explain that I'm an embedded journalist with Hammerspace, but Doom Machine cuts me off.

"This is unacceptable! We are mere days from the completion of the chaos engine and you bring a journalist into our secret lair! If I didn't know better I would suspect you were attempting to sabotage our plans, Schrodinger."

"You keep talkin' like that about my boy and I fin'a lay some beats down all over your ass," Ghettoblaster threatens back at Doom Machine.

"Your insolence is noted, human," Doom Machine says to Ghettoblaster as he approaches our group. "But the Schrodinger knows this is not the time for power plays or recruitment unless, of course, he planned this all along. Maybe HE killed Malo."

"That doesn't make any sense," says Principal Uncertainty as he also says "That makes perfect sense."

"Indeed, one possible outcome of Principal Uncertainty, perhaps the Schrodinger would be so kind as to provide his whereabouts last Tuesday."

"Wait, I thought ██████ killed El Malo Grande," interrupts Hammerspace.

Mr. Meltdown, who has been sitting silently in a corner until now erupts into laughter. "The ██████? Yeah. And afterward they met Bigfoot and the Loch Ness monster at Area 51 for tea," he says.

"Silencio!" says Dark Pope. His interpreter repeats "Silence, say his unholiness." He continues, through the interpreter. "The Pope say he know Mr. Schrodinger not kill El Malo Grande. Schrodinger was with him that day. But he do want to know why these strangers here."

The Schrodinger offers an explanation. "Since Hammerspace put General Welfare out of commission the superheroes have arranged a major team up to find him and rescue the General somehow. Should they succeed then they will once again be at full strength and, without the distraction of their missing comrade, much more likely to focus their efforts on us. So you see, it is in our best interest to keep them occupied elsewhere."

The Dark Pope nods quietly. He seems like a fair

guy, as supervillains go. Doom Machine says nothing.

Ghettoblaster speaks up. "That's the smartest thing I've heard all day."

Mr. Meltdown disagrees. "Come on. You can't seriously think we should sink resources into helping these costards."

Dark Pope rambles through his interpreter some more. "Dark Pope say Mr. Schrodinger have good idea."

"I must agree this time," roars Doom Machine. "Hiding Hammerspace should provide a worthwhile distraction."

"Well, now that that's settled I need one of you to take him in," says the Schrodinger.

"You've got to be kidding!" shouts Meltdown. "You find this idiot and bring him here without saying anything to any of us and then you try to shovel this shit onto one of us?"

"Scarlet Avenger saw me take them all with me," explains Schrodinger. "The super chumps are probably checking out my compound right now. It isn't safe. We need to hide Hammerspace with one of you."

Hammerspace seems angered. He interjects. "Who says I need help from any of you?"

"Don't be preposterous," replies Schrodinger. "When I found you the Avenger was beating you like a dirty throw rug."

"That was all part of my master plan."

"Right," chuckles Mr. Meltdown.

"You shut your pie hole, chucklehead," shouts Hammerspace. "Last I checked, you were showing a big fat zero win record against the superheroes. I remember General Welfare laying a smackdown on you that made the cover of Newsweek. Who took him out? Hmmm. Hmmmm. Was it....me?"

Indeed, he is correct. The August 2010 issue of Newsweek featured General Welfare bashing Mr. Meltdown in the face with his mighty fist of justice against the backdrop of the Statue of Liberty. Meltdown was thrown in jail afterwards and spent six weeks in solitary confinement before Doom Machine lasered his way into Riker's Island and flew him out. It took six weeks because Doom Machine was trapped at the bottom of the Mariana trench after Scarlet Avenger literally smacked him there (it was technically a backhand).

"Come to think of it, everyone in this room is oh and something except for me. Have any of you guys ever even killed a sidekick?"

The other villains in the room look around at each other awkwardly. It is Ghettoblaster who breaks the silent confusion. "Yeah. How come we haven't killed any of the superheroes?" he says.

"If we kill the superheroes then who will we have super battles against?" asks Schrodinger.

"Screw super battles. Let's get to the world domination part," says Ghettoblaster.

"Finally, somebody in this crew has some sense!" Hammerspace elates.

"Alexander wept for three days when he had no more worlds to conquer. I know. I was there," notes Schrodinger.

"Whatever. He was a three dollar bill. I say let's run this bitch."

"Dark Pope say he too old for world domination.

Maybe a large province somewhere," says the evil Pope's interpreter.

"How would we kill superheroes anyway?" asks Meltdown.

Ghettoblaster has the answer. "We could follow them home after a fight to see where they live and then we could bomb their house while they're sleeping or something."

"What if they have kids? I don't want to kill kids," says Ghettoblaster.

"And yet you support a woman's right to choose," scolds Meltdown as he rolls his eyes.

"So what?"

"His unholiness wishes to convey that what a woman does with her body is her business."

"Does anyone feel like getting sandwiches?" asks Principal Uncertainty.

"Subway or Quiznos?" someone says.

"You won't know until you have the sandwiches," replies Uncertainty.

"You know a fetus has a heartbeat at 18 days," says Meltdown.

"Google maps says Subway is closer. We could take the Deathbird."

"They charge extra for baco-"

"ENOUGH!" growls Doom Machine, rattling the walls of the conference room. "The chaos engine is mere days from completion and you squabble like children! Who will provide lodgings for Hammerspace?!"

"He can stay with me," offers Ghettoblaster.

"Good," says Doom Machine. "Then get these insects out of here!"

CHAPTER TWELVE

Ghettoblaster's hidden mansion fortress is enormous. Any number of times over the last few days I've found myself lost in the labyrinthine corridors. The walls are lavishly decorated in stolen art and solid gold busts of Ghettoblaster sit mounted on many surfaces. Curiously, the mansion's walls are amiss with dozens of gaping, man-sized holes smashed haphazardly through the dry wall. It is occasionally more convenient to walk through these to reach adjoining rooms, but in other places they appear right next to a door. I tried asking one of Ghettoblaster's henchmen about that, but he just said something nonsensical and bore his gold grill. I had a sit down with Ghettoblaster in front of an original painted version of The Scream.

"I got the solid gold bust idea from MC Hammer. I met him back in eighty nine when I was just a kid. He was huge back then. It was a different time," he says. "That was before gangsta became this giant thing that it is. Back then kids wanted to be something instead of being – well, what it is. It is what it is."

Is there anything that isn't what it is?

He stares at me for a moment stretching his mind and then he shakes his head and he says "What the hell is that suppose to mean? You playing games? Cause I don't play games."

I manage to shift the topic to the chaos engine.

"The chaos engine is this thing we're working on right now. Doom Machine has his people building it and we're gonna set it off to and it'll knock out all the electrical devices on the planet. So like computers, cell phones, radios – nothing's gonna work when we blow this shit up. Pretty much everything is gonna be screwed up. So then when people are running around not knowing how to do shit to take care of their situation, we can step in and take over everything."

But what about the superheroes?

"There's gonna be a huge crossover. I mean there's gonna be like fifteen superheroes fighting the chaos engine at least."

The chaos engine can fight?

"Yeah, we're putting it inside a giant robot so it can fly. The robot has rocket boots."

Couldn't you put it in a jet?

"See we thought of that, but then it couldn't fight the superheroes."

If the chaos engine makes machines stop working, and it's inside a robot, won't it make the robot stop working?

"I don't know. Doom Machine is building it. He's in charge of that stuff."

Later I find Hammerspace sitting on a huge leather sofa with his feet propped up on a marble coffee table in front of him. A White Russian sits on the table and a gigantic plasma screen TV mounted on the opposite wall plays a satellite feed of CNN. They've been covering the passage of the president's social equality bill in congress. A ton of supporters hold picket signs on capitol hill. Fumigator snores loudly from a reclining chair. Hammerspace writes in his tiny spiral notepad.

"I've just been chilling here coming up with ideas. There isn't much to do in this place really. Ghetto-blaster plays XBOX all day, but I've never been all that hot for video games," Hammerspace tells me. I sit down on the sofa. He jots something else down in his notepad. "It's sort of inspiring though."

"I've got this thing where I break into the Sony factory and alter all the alarm clocks to buzz with a sound that kills. I don't have a killing sound yet, so that's something that needs to be looked into. I'm also throwing around the idea of starting a company that manufactures adult diapers with mind control devices built in."

Why would you do that?

He shifts into his supervillain voice and growls "with the world's incontinent at my command I will be nigh unstoppable!" He shakes his fist and bares his teeth as he says the last of it. I spent five years getting my English degree and I have no idea what nigh means. I'm fairly certain Hammerspace doesn't either, but I suppose it works.

"The hardest part of the job really is coming up with original ideas. Everything has been done before

and that's a problem. Yeah, you can stick to the clas-
sics a lot of the time – throwing girls off buildings,
allying with the mole men, but you need to come up
with new things to keep the heroes on their toes. This
thing the League is doing with the giant robot has totally been done a thousand times by the way. Honestly, after what I've seen I'm kind of wondering why
anyone looks up to these guys. The Schrodinger's a
decent guy I guess. How about Doom Machine? He
doesn't stop. He's like one of those stand-up comics
that gets taken over by their stage persona and forgets
how to be normal. He's the Rodney Dangerfield of
evil."

He's very defensive about the notion that he may
have been inspired by the GCL villains in beginning
his career. "Yeah, they were around, but it's not like I
decided to go into the business so I could be like
them. I told you before I want power. I want to run
the show. I want to do what I want when I want and
have everyone else do what I say. Who doesn't want
that?"

He brings up an interesting point. Who hasn't
looked around at the way the world works and
thought that they could do it better? Even if for some
simple thing like the way traffic lights work or the
laws for child custody in Nevada, everyone believes
they could make everything run a little more smoothly
if they had their say. Normal people have to rally together in huge groups to accomplish the tiniest
changes, but for someone like Hammerspace or
Doom Machine it only takes a whim. That kind of
power must be intoxicating in a way I can't imagine.
He can take what he wants and make his own rules

and there is no one who can tell him otherwise – except for the superheroes. It must be truly infuriating to know that only a dozen people stand between yourself and unlimited personal gratification. Strangely, I feel I can relate to that sort of frustration. Stranger still, I question the motives of superheroes. What they do every day is like winning the lottery and giving all the money away to charity. Everything I know about human nature tells me it doesn't add up.

It is four o'clock in the afternoon when Ghettoblaster is called away to meet Doom Machine on business and he leaves us in the mansion alone with most of the henchmen. Fumigator wakes up hungry and complains that he can't find any food and so some of the henchmen offer to take the HoMobile on a munchie run to the nearest gas station. Hammerspace and Fumigator provide them with a list of snacks to pick up which includes (among other things) Triscuits, frozen pizza, bean dip, and "those little sausage biscuit sandwiches that come frozen in plastic wrappers so that when you heat them up the cheese melts and you can't get them out of the packaging." The henchmen quickly conclude that many of these items will be unavailable at the small food mart and they will have to travel to a much larger grocery farther away.

After they leave, the Schrodinger shows up looking for Ghettoblaster. We tell him Ghettoblaster was called away and he says he'll sit with us and wait for him to come back. Hammerspace laments forgetting to tell the henchmen to get pre-sliced pepperonis for his Triscuits. He notes the convenience of having the henchmen around. "You know, before I was skeptical about the whole henchmen thing, but I have to say, staying here has really changed my mind on that one. These guys are great. Remind me to ask Ghettoblaster about pay scale."

I'm way ahead of him on this one. "We pay most of our henchmen a yearly salary," says Edna Davis, Ghettoblaster's human resources manager. "Hanging around the fortress all day can add up overtime expenses really fast and we need to avoid that, but there are some cases where we pay an hourly rate – if we hire an assassin or an engineer we pay hourly for special projects like that." And what about health care in a line of work where one could (very likely) be crushed by a five storey dinobot or lasered in half by a meltaray? "The company offers full health benefits with dental, although they don't cover cosmetic dentistry."

It is four forty five when Black Bandit comes crashing through the skylight in Ghettoblaster's den. He destroys a glass coffee table underfoot as he lands in a shower of falling glass shards. The dark cloaked superhero opens his cape wide to reveal a ripped frame covered in black body armor. His pecks are like Arnold's and his six pack is more like a twenty six pack. He whips his arm and launches a whole volley of razor sharp bandit blades at the Schrodinger, who stands by the bar pouring himself another drink. The Schrodinger takes a huge blade in the face and slumps dead over the bar.

"That's for what you did to Scarlet Avenger," says the Black Bandit in a low rasp before turning his attention to Hammerspace. "Now, tell me what you've done to General Welfare!"

A henchman bursts into the room and shrieks "Not the skylight! Blaster's gonna be pissed!" Then the Black Bandit smacks him in the head with an end table.

Hammerspace laughs. "And if I don't talk then what? You're outnumbered and outgunned, Black Buttwipe!"

"Not for long, Hammerslob!" says Black Bandit.

That instant, Commander Commando smashes through an exterior wall and steps into the den. He is tall and wears an orange and black get-up with a green visor covering his eyes. "This looks like a job for POWER TEAM!" he bellows. Following him are Lightning Guy and Bullet Time.

Fumigator leaps up and shakes his finger at Commander Commando. "You can't touch me! You aren't supposed to come within five hundred feet! You know what the judge said!"

"The judge ain't here, bud. And this ol' dog's itchin' to kick your ass," says Wombat as he crashes in through a window alongside Miss Frigid.

Fumigator and Hammerspace both scream like girls. This isn't flattering, and they will likely deny it, but I have it on tape. Hammerspace actually yells, "We're dead! We're dead! They're gonna kill us! We're dead!"

That's when there is a deafening bang and the room flashes a blinding bright white. I can't hear anything over the ringing in my ears. Someone shoves me to the ground. I force my eyes open and I make out a dark figure kicking Black Bandit across the room. Something huge picks up Commander Commando and swings him into Wombat like a Louisville Slugger.

SUPERVILLAINOUS!

I feel around in the dissonant wreckage. I think Hammerspace is yelling at me. The ringing slowly decreases in volume to the level of noise in the room and then below. I find that I am pinned under an unconscious Fumigator. Hammerspace is being dragged away by a giant armored monster of some kind. It growls "Flesh for my hunger."

I can't move to follow them, but somehow, and I don't usually think this quickly, I have the presence of mind to toss Hammerspace my tape recorder. He catches it in his outstretched hand and vanishes into the void.

CHAPTER THIRTEEN

As the smoke clears, I find myself standing in the middle of Ghettoblaster's ruined den. Fumigator is nowhere to be seen (I would later learn he slipped out in the confusion and escaped down a storm drain). Superheroes lie scattered about the room in varied states of consciousness and there are now several more holes smashed in the drywall. Wombat is the first to approach me.

"Who the hell is this guy?" he says, gruffly, as if I'm not right there listening to him.

I tell him I'm an embedded journalist with the supervillains and he almost laughs. Commander Commando does laugh. The Black Bandit is much more serious. After he yells at me for a while and asks a bunch of questions I don't have answers to, he is reprimanded by Commander Commando. They get into a heated round of aggressive posturing, in which Power Team backs up Commando and Black Bandit exclaims "This isn't over, Commando," before throwing down a smoke bomb and vanishing. I really need to find out how they do that.

Commander Commando says I should stop following these costards and see how a real super team operates. Wombat scoops up the Schrodinger's cadaver and we end up on Power Team's ZX joint strike super shuttle. Before long we're setting down on their landing pad high atop the Power Tower in Los Angeles. Bullet Time tells me about their world famous base of operations as we set down.

"We built the Power Tower in ninety-nine entirely out of pocket. The bottom thirty floors are office complexes, a three floor shopping mall, parking structure, a movie theater - there's a concert venue somewhere in there too. Then floors thirty-one through forty belong to R and D, our legal department, merchandising, all that stuff. The top ten floors are sealed off and those are just ours. We have multiple living quarters and all of the world's most prominent superheroes live here. Aside from Power Team, Scarlet Avenger, The Nightstick, and Fire Dancer, even though she's retired, are just some of the heroes living in the Power Tower."

The inside of the Power Team's compound makes Ghettoblaster's mansion look like a studio apartment back home in Cincinnati. Just walking around I find a video arcade and pool room, an indoor pool, a movie theater, a sauna, a shooting range and another video arcade. There are several areas I cannot access and I can only assume these are dedicated to war rooms, super computers, armories and other super necessities.

"Being a superhero definitely has its bonuses. For

all the work we do, we really do get a lot back from the community," says Commander Commando as he plays an original coin-op Metal Slug arcade machine. What kind of work does a superhero do exactly?

"Patrolling? No. Not really so much. It actually doesn't yield results like on TV. You can patrol all night, your chances of actually stumbling onto a robbery in progress or a violent rape is[sic] pretty low," says Commando. "I think that happened to me once and that's it." At least twice, actually. I found the newspaper articles.

"We usually handle the big stuff around here - calls from the president or the Pentagon or MI6. This General Welfare thing has really got everybody going. I'm not that worried though. Hammerspace is a third rate class two villain. He tries way too hard and he doesn't follow the rules. He's a loose cannon. He's going to get screwed in the end. Guys like that always do. You have to play ball."

Play ball?

"Yeah. You can't do the kind of shit he's doing. Killing a guy's sidekick during a kids show? With a gun? What kind of guy does that? There wasn't even a fair fight. He just pulled out a gun and shot him. There should be laws against that kind of thing."

Isn't that felony murder one?

"Is it? Hot damn. You may be on to something," says Commando as he whips up a wall-mounted phone and asks someone named Stan in legal to look into it for him.

Who do you think grabbed Hammerspace anyway?

"Alls[sic] I know is they were incredibly powerful

if they overpowered my whole team and the Black Bandit. It could have been Doom Machine and El Malo Grande."

El Malo Grande is dead.

"Really? When did that happen? Oh well. No one stays dead long in this business."

I follow Commander Commando down to a lower floor where he strips off most of his clothes in front of a team of sculptors who take plaster casts of his limbs for a new action figure. The process takes hours and through most of it he rants to me about how he didn't know anything about quality until he discovered PRS guitars. Also he insists he's going to show me his new pipe once he finishes. I manage to slip out while he's arguing with someone about whether the variant figures should have a blue or cyan costume.

I begin roaming the hallways of Power Tower in search of a Pepsi machine so that I might partake of a delicious Mountain Dew soda beverage. After fifteen minutes I manage to find a machine a few floors up. After another five minutes is spent force feeding a badly crinkled dollar bill into the machine, I have a can of pop which I sip as I meander back down the hallway dreading the thought of Commander Commando showing me his boring drug paraphernalia. I've only made it a few steps from the Pepsi machine when I hear the sound of a woman crying. Curiosity gets the better of me (pretty easily considering the alternative) and I decide to investigate. I take a corner and a flying cell phone nearly kills me. I feel it graze my ear before I know what it is and I have to turn and look back at the phone, which is actually embedded in the drywall, to tell what type of missile I nearly had rammed through my brain.

Very quickly an upset young woman is doting over me and apologizing for nearly spearing my face with a Nokia. She is tall and remarkably attractive. She brushes her long and shiny red hair back as she wipes her eyes and introduces herself in a thick British accent. We'll call her Susie. Susie is the Scarlet Avenger.

I'm not saying Susie told me in exactly so many words that she's the Scarlet Avenger, but it was certainly implied and, at times, painfully obvious. This mask thing doesn't work nearly as well as they think it does.

After her long string of apologies has ended I start working her over with some superpowers of my own. We head down to the building lounge where we get a table near a mediocre saxophone player. Cocktails are nearly ten dollars. I open a tab I know I'll regret later and start asking questions.

I find out Susie threw a Nokia 5800 at my head because her boyfriend, whom we'll call Rick, told her it wasn't working out and they should probably just be friends. "I felt like I had finally met 'the one', you know?" she says as she knocks back her fourth margarita in twenty minutes. She remains completely sober. "It's so hard meeting guys who aren't full of rubbish and I have this job – it's very high pressure and I don't have time to meet people and the men I work with are… What I do is a very male dominated profession. I don't know if you figured it out yet, but if you know then you know. And it's especially weird because I'm the best there is in my field and men are afraid of me. They are. If they're not afraid then they're jealous or they resent me. So I can't see guys in my line of work and I can't meet guys outside and for Christ's sake I'm thirty two! The clock is ticking. You know? But Rick didn't know what I do and that was working. It was great because I could go out with him and just feel like a girl again. You know? But then out of the blue he just dumps me. Why? Is there something wrong with me? Is that what that means? I thought it was the job thing getting in my way but maybe not. Maybe I'm just not the kind of girl men want."

I try to be consoling, but as anyone who knows me will tell you, consoling is not something I can do. I read in a magazine that women appreciate a good listener and that sounds like an easy strategy so I just shut up and occasionally nod and agree with whatever Susie is talking about. She is remarkably uninteresting. She talks constantly about her crazy cats. Their names are Mittens and Gandalf. Mittens is black with white paws and Gandalf is (surprise) grey. After half a dozen margaritas and a ton of this cat talk, she still hasn't left the table to pee. I don't know exactly what that means, but I can tell you it isn't normal.

When I buy the seventh or eighth round I order a chocolate mudslide ($11.50) for myself which I insist is the best mudslide I have ever had and push across the table for Susie to try. Three times I attempt this and three times she turns me down. She seems agitated the third time and she glares at me. She says "Is this the game you want to play?" I grin and ask her whatever she could possibly mean by that. That's when I feel her foot sliding up my leg under the table. She asks if I'd like to see her apartment.

Her apartment is positively radical. In a way it reminds me of Hammerspace's crib back in Jersey because there are tons of bizarre items displayed on tables and mantles. I notice a jet pack, a magic lamp, half of a moon laser and what appears to be one of Doom Machine's arms (he must be able to replace damaged parts). The difference is that Susie's apartment is infinitely classier than Hammerspace's and includes a balcony view of the entire city. It is also immaculately clean. Come to think of it, it isn't at all like Hammerspace's apartment.

As she closes the door behind us I make my usual go-to move, which is shoving her against the door and sticking my tongue in her mouth (yeah, I'm that kind of guy). The problem is that pushing her is like pushing a skyscraper. She doesn't budge. She stands for a second eyeing me with confusion and then she awkwardly feigns being pushed back into the door. This is emasculating to an unimaginable degree and my confidence is completely wrecked. I should have realized earlier that I am entirely too neurotic to ever get it up for the world's hottest superheroine. I tell her I don't think I can do this. She drops her top on the floor and bites her bottom lip. Suddenly I'm not at all concerned about performance issues.

Things heat up pretty fast. I strip most of her clothes off right there on the floor and we roll around for a while making out. I can tell she's more nervous than she lets on because she kisses poorly. She has a tendency to peck around without really committing to anything, which is especially obnoxious because I can't hold her in place. She's too strong. She keeps saying she doesn't usually do this kind of thing and she doesn't want me to think she's that type of girl. Eventually she stops and says "I need something to loosen up a little bit." She walks over to the kitchen wearing nothing but her scarlet cotton panties and a pair of socks and retrieves a bottle of prescription medication and a full handle of vodka from on top of the refrigerator. She eats a bunch of pills like she's emptying a packet of Pez and tips that handle like a water bottle. I watch her perfect breasts bounce ever so slightly with each massive gulp as she consumes the entire handle. Then she slides her panties to the floor and beckons for me to follow her to the bedroom.

The Scarlet Avenger is a pill-popping, alcoholic, neurosis-stricken, self-loathing, mass of insecurities. She is also amazing in the sack.

CHAPTER FOURTEEN

The following is a transcript of the tape I recovered from Hammerspace after the incident at the Ghettomansion. He was able to keep the recorder in his jacket where it continued to record until the battery ran out. Names have been attached to voices where possible. Certain portions have been blacked out at the request of my editor, who was not threatened in any way by any organizations existent or non-existent, past or present. Such a non-existent organization certainly did not threaten to kill his kids. I also must state that the identities of the individuals on the tape and their affiliations are unknown, again at the request of my editor.

The sound of a helicopter engine made the first few minutes of the tape very difficult or impossible to understand. Most of it has been left out of this printing to save paper.

SUPERVILLAINOUS!

Unknown Male: (unintelligible)....like I'm back in.....(unintelligible) gimme shelter on a (unintelligible) hundred yards (laughing)

Unknown Male: (unintelligible) tape recorder

████: Burn him 'till he (unintelligible)

████: Set down here!

Hammerspace: I've got (a) thermal detonator in here!

████: Shut up!

████: There's no (unintelligible) thermal (unintelligible)

████: (growling)

The engine noise fades.

Hammerspace: I swear I'll blow us all to kingdom come!

████: Nobody cares. Close your jacket. You look like you're flashing a playground.

Hammerspace: I'm not giving you General Welfare!

████: Fine. Keep him. The guy's a banana.

Hammerspace: Lies! No one fools Hammerspace! Not even ████████!

███: We're not ████████████.

Hammerspace: What?

████: We're ██████████████, ya bloody poofter.

Hammerspace: What the hell? I'm on the verge of world domination here and ████████ sends their second stringers? Why don't I get ██████████? El Malo Grande got ██████████...

████: No. That was us too. ██████████████ doesn't operate anymore.

Lonnie: ██████████████████

Hammerspace: ████████████████████? That doesn't make any sense. How is it a██████████████ ████████

████: Trust me. If you saw, you'd understand.

Hammerspace: Then you killed El Malo Grande! Fools! Prepare yourselves to be crushed by the awesome power of Hammerspace!

████████: Wrong again.

Unknown Male: Malo was working for us. We were trying to save him.

Hammerspace: What?

SUPERVILLAINOUS!

███████: I told you this was a bad idea, ██████. Let me burn him. None of this noisy shit. Just a slow burn. Makes a soft crackle. Relaxing sound. Makes you feel warm inside.

Unknown Male: Yes, ██████. Fire makes things warm.

Hammerspace: He doesn't seem particularly balanced.

██████: We're very good at what we do, Mr. Thompson. Being very good at what we do comes at an enormous social cost.

██████: Fresh meat.

██████: Yes, ██████. Meat.

Hammerspace: If you guys didn't kill Malo, then who did?

██████: Who else has the power to take out Malo?

Hammerspace: The superheroes?

██████: Wrong. How did the superheroes know where to find you?

Hammerspace: They must have planted a tracking device on me before. Blast you, heroes!

██████: No. I hate dealing with these costumed super idiots!

Hammerspace: Careful, simpleton! The fate of humanity, YOUR FATE, lies in our super hands!

█████: Please. You guys are street performers at best.

Hammerspace: We fight on the front lines of the eternal battle between good and evil, the battle for domination of the world!

█████: You put on a show in ridiculous spandex tights while the real deal is going on under the table. But that's fine. We welcome the distraction. Now let's try this again. I'll dumb it down a lot for you this time. Who called Ghettoblaster to get him out of the house right before the superheroes showed up?

Hammerspace: Doom Machine?

█████: And who do you think also told the superheroes where to find you?

Hammerspace: Doom Machine!

█████: And who killed El Malo Grande?

Hammerspace: Doom Machine... Why would Doom Machine kill El Malo Grande?

Unknown Asian Male: Because he found out about the chaos engine.

Hammerspace: So what? I know about the chaos engine. We all know about the chaos engine.

██████: Except you think it's an EMP generator constructed to knock out all of the planet's electronic devices.

Hammerspace: Yeah…

██████: ████████████, do your thing.

████████████: The chaos engine is a phase amplification synoptic conversion array designed to generate maximum effervescence of moored civil constructs.

Hammerspace: Oh. Now that you put it that way.

Unknown Male: It's a riot machine. You flip a switch. Everybody on the planet starts killing everybody else around them.

Hammerspace: Why would Doom Machine…

██████: Because he's an alien! They sent him here to wipe us out! Look, it doesn't matter. Here's the low down. We can't have Doom Machine running the show, so we're putting you in charge. Supervillains will work for you and you're gonna work for us.

Hammerspace: Fools! Hammerspace is a pawn of no one!

██████: ██████, eat his fingers.

███████: (growling)

Hammerspace: Whoa! Whoa. Whoa. We don't need to eat any fingers.

███████: I thought you would see things my way.

███████: (growling)

██████: ██████, back off.

█████: Hunger!

███████: Remember the Iranian family in lock up? Yeah. If you're good, you can eat the baby when we get back to base.

██████: Baby?

Hammerspace: Oh shit.

██████: Yeah. Baby... Yeah. There you go. Put him down.

Hammerspace: Wait, why me?

██████: You took out a class three superhero by yourself. We were sort of impressed.

Hammerspace: So I work for you guys - who do you guys work for?

Unknown Male: ████████████████

Hammerspace: Huh. At least it's not the lizard people.

████████: What do you know about lizard people?

Hammerspace: Nothing. Just what Skullf- wait, what?

████████████: That's a good sign. We were worried about the potential for fourth dimensional perforation occurring as a side effect of his abilities, but it looks like a ten dimensional construct is a more valid explanation now.

Hammerspace: So how did he do it anyway? I thought Grande was invincible.

██████: Turns out he could still drown.

Hammerspace: Murdered in his own swimming pool.

██████: A lava flow actually.

Hammerspace: Oh wow. Now THAT'S how you kill a guy!

████████: I'll burn you, you stupid git!

██████: Back off, █████!

████████: █ and █████ melted alive in that lava flow!

██████: Casualties happen! You need to keep it together! Christ, I've never seen you like this. You were sleeping with her weren't you?

██████ : None of your God damn business!

██████ : We lost two of our team in there with Malo. Doom Machine is… very dangerous.

Hammerspace: I never would have guessed.

██████ : We need to-

End of tape.

CHAPTER FIFTEEN

I wake up in the Scarlet Avenger's bed. She's nowhere to be found so I walk down the hallway to use her bathroom. I take a peek in her medicine cabinet while I'm in there. I find quite a few bottles of Lithium, some Respidol, Plan B, a straight razor, condoms, amyl nitrate, and a syringe.

I decide the best thing to do is pick my clothes up and leave. By the time I get dressed and open the front door she's standing there in the hallway. "Were you trying to escape?" she says. Then she giggles nervously. I insist I was just going out to find a newspaper and she tells me she has it delivered and points to a paper on a table inside the apartment.

I end up having breakfast with her. She can't do much in the kitchen, so I make omelets. I can never manage to flip an omelet over properly. I always end up dashing the whole thing to pieces in the process and then I have to just pile all the chunks on a plate and pretend I did it right. The Avenger thinks this is cute. In fact, she makes kind of a big deal about it, way more than any normal person should care about.

We finish breakfast and she's ready for sex again. She backs me onto this little love seat in her front room and says "You're the most incredible lover I've ever been with, Michael. I want to snort you like cocaine. Let's make a baby."

I tell her I have an appointment at whatever time it is right now. I can be a pretty convincing liar. She gives me a wink and tells me to hurry back. I get the hell out of her apartment.

Wombat is in the elevator. He laughs at me like he knows exactly what just happened. "You know she's bipolar as hell, right?" he says. Then he adds, "At least you wrapped it up." That he knows all of this frightens me at first. Then I surmise he's able to tell me these things because of his superhuman sense of smell. He's quiet and doesn't say much else all the way down to the lobby.

The elevator doors ding open and Commander Commando is standing in the lobby answering questions for a gathering of reporters. "We're doing everything in our power to find General Welfare and bring the evildoers to justice. Power Team spent the entire day yesterday combing the world over in search of the villains responsible." It's funny because I remember him playing an expensive Neo Geo video game for most of the day.

I sneak past the Commander, but on my way out the doors Bullet Time catches up to me and asks if I'd take a look at the spec script he just wrote for a biopic about him starring him as himself. "It's a really deep story and I think I have a lot to say that, well, you know I'm really ahead of so many people intellectually and I want to get some things out there," he says as we walk and talk. "I'm just hoping to get another screenwriter's take on it." I'm reluctant to answer as these types of requests usually lead to a damned if you do scenario. Screenplays are almost universally awful, especially ones written by amateurs. If I read it and tell him it sucks he'll hate me. If I refuse to read it, he'll hate me. If I lie and say it's good, then he'll pester me to help him get exposure and then my reputation is on the line. I'm trying to navigate these dark waters when I hear a scream from a nearby alley. I ask Bullet Time if we should investigate and he says he has a meeting in two minutes with Jim Cameron. He keeps walking. I head down the alley and find some kids joking around. It's nothing, but if it were something then Bullet Time would have really dropped the ball.

I make a call to Larry from a payphone in a grocery store. This is after walking up and down Wilshire for twenty minutes asking people if they know where to find a payphone. Larry screams at me as soon as he picks up the phone. He's infuriated. He can't believe I'm in LA. He can't believe I've been following supervillains for this long. He's mad at me for not getting an exclusive with the Scarlet Avenger. I tell him I was already as exclusive as I'd ever want to be with her. I promise him recordings of Doom Machine's actual voice. He thinks maybe we could sell those to a tabloid. I leave out that I lost my tape recorder when mysterious boogeymen dragged Hammerspace away. I guess I'll cross my fingers on getting that back.

I end up walking into a McDonalds for lunch on a

pretty down note. I've followed supervillains for weeks now and I've only been let down more and more. There haven't been any battles with giant killer robots or intergalactic invaders. No one has activated a doomsday machine only to have the world's super-heroes join forces to stop them. There have been no damsels in distress. I haven't seen anything particularly adventurous at all. What little action I have seen has been carried out (mostly by Hammerspace) with a ferocity reminiscent of a gangland drive-by shooting. None of these people are anything like the archetypes they represent and they certainly aren't exemplary human beings. The superheroes are the worst part of the whole scene. They're vain, narcissistic, and slovenly. Commander Commando is a complete douche bag. The Scarlet Avenger is insane. None of them seem to spend any time actually helping people. Of course, they'll show up to smack Hammerspace around for some publicity, but that's in their own interest. I have a little more respect for the villains who, despite being admittedly evil, actually work to accomplish something. Hammerspace is constantly jotting down notes and planning and attempting world domination. Maybe his plans don't make a lot of sense and his ultimate goal is not desirable by most of the world but he works hard at it every single day – and loves what he does. That's more than I can say for Commander Dickhead, whom I have seen doing little else but smoking weed and playing video games.

All of this is compounded when the runt at the counter tells me they don't sell chicken nuggets anymore. Apparently something in the social equality bill that just passed enacts enormous taxes on any restaurants serving fried food. McDonalds can no longer afford to sell McNuggets. I tell the clerk I'll have a number one instead. He reads a surgeon general's warning against eating grilled beef products and then asks me if I'm sure. I tell him yes – but with more expletives.

In the afternoon I board a jet back home to Cincinnati and basically give up on the whole project. It takes three hours to get through airport security. I'm on the plane for another four. By the time I get a rental and get back to my place, I'm wishing I had a joint strike super shuttle like Power Team. I walk in the door pretty angry, but mainly just wanting to fall down in bed, turn the TV to something mindless and fall asleep.

I'm totally surprised when Hammerspace is waiting in my kitchen. He's sitting in a chair eating Fruity Pebbles in chocolate soy milk. He tells me I'm out of regular milk. I ask him what he's doing in my house. His face lights up in this massive grin I'll never forget and he says "The shit just got real."

CHAPTER SIXTEEN

"First thing, it's Baron Hammerspace now. I've been given a barony by my mysterious benefactors," Hammerspace – Baron Hammerspace says. "It's in Nigeria somewhere. I heard it's a hellhole. I don't know."

I stare at him curiously waiting for the next thing.

"Next, things are about to get real crazy and I need you to be my official journalist. The official journalist of Baron Hammerspace."

I ask him for more information.

"There's no time to explain! We have to get to the Hammerhead!"

I tell him I'm ready to go.

"Hang on. Let me finish my pebbles."

He takes five minutes to finish his pebbles and then he pours himself another bowl. I sit down at the table after a few minutes. Hammerspace comments about my trip to LA. "So, the Scarlet Avenger, I heard you tapped that. Is it true the, uh, carpet doesn't match the drapes?" I tell him I'm not sure. There was all wood flooring - if you know what I mean. He doesn't get it. I'm not in the mood to explain. I can't believe he heard about that already. "Everybody knows. She's really pissed. She told Ms. Frigid she's going to throw you across the international dateline. Would that be yesterday or tomorrow from this direction? I always forget." Hell hath no fury...

Eventually he finishes the pebbles. Then he jumps up from his seat and yells "to the Hammerhead!" I follow him out the front door and around the block and we jump in his rental car and drive to the airport. At the airport we board the Hammerhead, Hammerspace's Gulfstream 3 jet. He tells me about the jet as we head down to the tarmac. "Behold, my flying base of operations! The constantly moving home to the world's greatest criminal mastermind! It used to belong to Miley Cyrus, but she sold it when the G5 came out. I found a stack of autographed photos in the overhead carry-on and a pair of Billy Ray's old boots. It could use a custom paint job — something with a lot of skulls I think."

Aboard the plane, Fumigator sits drinking a martini next to three new super characters I've never seen or heard of before. One is a pretty blonde girl wearing a black tee shirt with a big yellow smiley face on it. The other is decked out in full Ku Klux Klan regalia to the point where I can't tell if it is male or female. The third is a guy in his early thirties with his hair gelled and a pair of seven hundred dollar sunglasses. Hammerspace introduces me. "Before you sit the members of my team — the Smiley Face Killer, legendary slayer of frat boys all across the American heartland. Beside her is the White Knight - master of the dreaded white power! Last but not least, Salesman, able to sell anything to anyone! Fumigator you already know. Together we form the dreaded Fiendish Five, bane of all that is just and bringers of doom to the legions of do-gooders that seek to stop us on our quest for world domination!" Then he cackles.

I can't honestly say I'm surprised Hammerspace is running his own crew now. The guy certainly has ambition. The only thing I've seen him lacking is direction, and now it seems some mysterious outfit has provided him with one. The plane is in the air within minutes and I have no idea where we're going. It doesn't matter for now. I get plenty of face time with the new guys.

The Smiley Face Killer is one of those bizarre urban legends you hear about but nobody really believes in. Supposedly, the killer lures college age men from bars all over the united states somehow and then drowns them in nearby bodies of water – always sure to leave a tell tale smiley face sticker somewhere in the immediate area as a grim calling card. Here's my Q&A with the killer.

Mike Leon: So, you're a girl?

Smiley Face Killer: Last I checked.

ML: Everybody who believes in you at all thinks you're a man.

SFK: I don't understand that. How do they think I lure those boys out of the bars? It isn't that hard to connect the dots.

ML: It really isn't.

SFK: It's a man's world.

ML: So do you have a super power?

SFK: I do. I'm super strong.

ML: Really? I would have guessed something more outlandish.

SFK: Everybody does. It's just male chauvinism. You all think the same way. Only men can have the good powers. Women have to turn invisible or be psychic or something lame and subtle.

ML: I don't agree. I'm very afraid of the Scarlet Avenger right now and there's nothing subtle about her.

SFK: She's confident. Men can't stand a woman in power. They have to turn her into a monster to bring her down.

ML: I see. So is that why all the gruesome murders?

SFK: Mostly.

The Salesman is considerably more talkative. "I figured it out while I was working in a Circuit City – this was way back when there still was a Circuit City.

Anyway, I kept telling customers to buy stuff and they would. I was selling five times as much stuff as anyone else in the store and I just figured I was a really good salesman, but then I realized how ridiculous it really was when I started comparing notes with other sales guys from other stores. Once I figured it out it was a no-brainer to quit that job and move on to cars and then I branched out into just about everything from there."

The White Knight interrupts with "Can I get a white power? Yee haw!" Everyone else on the plane stops for a second and then the Smiley Face Killer accuses him of being a racist. White Knight shrugs.

A few minutes later the Salesman spits into a napkin and sells it to the Smiley Face Killer for six dollars. He then uses the six dollars to tip one of the stewardesses (Yes, the Hammerhead has stewardesses). "I can only sell tangible objects – goods not services," elaborates the Salesman. "And it's really difficult to get around it. I found out when I tried to sell, quote, my nuts, end quote, to a girl at the Viper Room. She came at me with a meat cleaver. The Toxic Shocker had to zap her pretty hardcore."

Apparently the Salesman also knows this Toxic Shocker guy. "Yeah, we did a bunch of jobs together down in Miami and then he ended up getting mixed up in this Eastern European thing and I haven't seen him for a while." He discredits rumors of a ███████ connection. "Yeah. He told me stuff like that. It's all bullshit. The Shocker's an okay guy and all. It's just he likes to tell tall tales and the weed doesn't help. You know? He's a little off. He told me this ridiculous story one time about how he was working with ███████ and he saw one of them kill a werewolf with a toothbrush or something. No part of that story makes sense. Assuming a werewolf did exist, which it doesn't, how would you kill it with a toothbrush? Isn't the whole thing with werewolves silver bullets? The shocker isn't exactly world class super agent material either. The idea that he's a top guy for a secret super army that enforces a global shadow agenda is pretty tough to swallow."

Hammerspace cuts into the conversation and announces that we will be arriving at the destination in an hour and he wants to start briefing the team on his plan. He pulls a projector from his jacket which he projects toward the back of the plane and then spends ten minutes fighting with Microsoft Powerpoint before he tosses the projector angrily aside and draws pictures on a napkin with a ball point pen. I know I'm curious about where it is we're going exactly.

"If we're going to wrest control of the Global Crime League then we must first destroy Doom Machine," Hammerspace begins. "To kill him we need to find him. To find him we need the Schrodinger. Only the Schrodinger knows the location of Doom Machine's lair."

"Question," interjects the Salesman. "Are the Stewardesses clean?"

"What? What does that even mean- oh. Oh. I don't know. Ask them."

"Do we really need whores on the plane?" says the Smiley Face Killer.

"What about the niggers and the Jews?" asks The White Knight.

"What the hell? Does anybody have any questions

about what we're actually doing?" yells Hammerspace. Heads shake. I'm the only one who has questions. He has to lay everything out for me and it takes about a half hour.

Apparently it goes like this: The GCL has been manipulated by Doom Machine into building the Chaos Engine, a device which will spell destruction for the entire human race so that beings from Doom Machine's home dimension can take over. He has accomplished this by disguising the Chaos Engine as a giant robot for the GCL to use in one of their giant crossover events. Malo found out what was really going on and he had to be removed from the picture followed by the Schrodinger, Doom Machine's chief rival for leadership of the GCL. Now Doom Machine has wrested control of the group and is pushing the completion of the Chaos Engine. Hammerspace has recruited a crack team of powerful supervillains to wrest control of the GCL and destroy Doom Machine. He has planned this with help from the CIA – he claims.

Just as I'm getting the idea what's going on the pilot comes on the overhead and says we're getting close. Hammerspace stands up from his seat and pulls a parachute pack from his jacket. He tosses it to Fumigator and says, "We need to get ready. We jump in ten."

CHAPTER SEVENTEEN

Jumping out of a plane is absolutely insane. I can think of nothing dumber I have ever done or even thought about doing. I've had friends who went sky-diving for recreational purposes and I didn't approve of it then either. It's just stupid.

"We're pretty low, so you'll want to pull that cord pretty much as soon as you're out of the plane," says Fumigator. I barely have time to protest before he pushes me out of the plane. I fumble around looking for the cord for about fifteen seconds and then I pull on it to extend the chute. I worry that the guards might shoot at us on our way down, but that fear turns out to be unfounded. I look back and see the rest of the team coming down behind me. The White Knight looks like a massive puff of billowing marsh-mallow lost in his white robes.

I hit the ground first in the middle of the prison yard during recess or workout time or whatever they call it when you're in prison and you're not locked in a cell. I stand up and look around at all the prison gangs divided into separate sectors of the yard. The blacks are laughing at me. The whites look angry. The Hispanic gang looks really suspicious and they keep whispering to each other in Spanish. I'm not liking this at all.

Hammerspace is next to hit the ground, followed by Fumigator. "Take them out," barks the Baron. Fumigator launches gas grenades into the crowds of inmates. Hammerspace tosses me a gas mask. Then he pulls a machine gun and starts mowing down the prison trash that gets too close to us. In a few more seconds the rest of the team is on the ground with us.

The doors to the prison yard smash open and a full team of riot geared police with sub machine guns and gas masks rush through. They're screaming at us to put our hands in the air. One guy keeps screaming "Interlace your fingers!" over and over. Hammerspace does nothing. Fumigator seems confused. I have no idea what to do. Then The White Knight points at a group of black inmates lying on the ground from the effects of Fumigator's gas and he yells "They did it!"

All of the riot cops charge the black gang and begin beating them furiously with night sticks. I can only guess this is the dreaded white power Hammerspace mentioned earlier. I ask Hammerspace what that was and he says "The White Knight's mere presence makes all the white people around him violently racist." I tell Hammerspace that doesn't make sense because I've been around The White Knight for a few hours now and I still don't have anything against niggers, wops, chinks, spics, or kikes. Especially the kikes. God damn Jews. Hammerspace laughs at me. I guess I didn't even realize it until now. I hope this is temporary.

I follow the Fiendish Five into the actual prison facility and we leave the guards to continue beating on the porch monkeys out in the yard. We head down a corridor and meet up with a dot head guard standing in our way. Can you believe that? The most dangerous criminals in the country and we have a damn dot head guarding them. What's next? Do we put the camel jockeys in charge of the nuclear missile silos?

The guard raises his gun and tells us to stop where we are and then Smiley Face Killer punches right through his head. She actually gets his head stuck around her bicep and has to jimmy it back down the length of her arm scowling the whole time as nasty hadji slime oozes all over her. She finally frees herself and then kicks down the steel door the towel head was guarding. The team charges through the door.

We've actually entered one of the main cell blocks, although I'm not sure which one, and most of the cells are empty. We pass a guy mopping the floor and when he sees us coming he leaps into a cell and locks himself in.

Before we're made it all the way through the cell block another group of guards bursts through the doors pointing automatic rifles at us. They open fire. Hammerspace ducks into an open cell and I follow him. The rest of the team jumps into another cell across the corridor. This is the first time I've been shot at with machine guns, and it's a little unnerving actually. Hammerspace returns fire with a heavy machine gun that looks like it should be mounted on a tank. After a few moments we're still pinned down and he doesn't seem to be making any progress.

The Salesman whips around the corner and holds up an object he grabbed from the cell to display to the guards shooting at us. "Hey guys, I'll sell you this, um, September 1998 issue of Vibe magazine for all of your guns," he says.

Immediately they all come out of hiding. They fork over their guns to the Salesman. One of them even excitedly remarks that Usher is on the cover of the magazine. Once he gives them the magazine they become considerably less enthused. Apparently the Salesman can sell anything, but he can't keep you wanting it after you have it. It doesn't matter because Fumigator points out that there are a bunch of coons causing trouble for our Aryan brothers outside and the guards go running to help. White power!

A few minutes later we're smashing our way into the solitary confinement room where they keep the Schrodinger. Smiley Face Killer kicks down a three-inch steel door and we walk into a sterile looking white room with no windows. There is a gurney in the center of the room on which sits the Schrodinger's body. A pair of guards sit hunched over the Schrodinger's corpse staring at it. I imagine they do this in shifts. Fumigator dispatches them both with some kind of toxic nerve gas spray and they shrivel to the floor.

We all stand over Schrodinger's body for a moment. Hammerspace scratches his head briefly and wonders aloud how to go about reviving the infamously immortal supervillain. Then the Smiley Face

Killer shouts "hey guys, look at my tits!" All she does is give us the finger though, and when we turn back to the Schrodinger he's hopping up off the gurney. He has two questions for us right away.

"Where am I? Have we wrested control of the world from the Zionists yet?" I tell him he's in a prison and the master race still struggles against the Jew conspiracy that secretly controls the government.

"Jew dogs!" he yells.

"You guys realize Judaism is a religion, not a race, right?" asks the Smiley Face Killer.

"I don't think it matters," says Hammerspace. "White Knight makes us hate all kinds of people. I kind of want to burn Catholics right now too. Bunch of child molesters. Everyone knows Catholicism is the false word. You cannot enter the kingdom of heaven based on good works alone."

"Actually, my powers don't work against Catholics," says the White Knight. "It's just Jews and colored people."

"Wow," says Hammerspace. "Are you sure?"

"Yeah. Completely."

"Well, that's um… weird then."

I'll say.

The Schrodinger's next question makes more sense than his last one. "How did I get here?"

Hammerspace takes this one. "We were set up by Doom Machine. He killed Malo. The chaos engine is going to end life as we know it. I'm taking over the league to stop him and this is my team. Join us and rule over the world we conquer! Refuse and you will die! What will it be?"

"I cannot die, so that is an idle threat, but I already knew about Doom Machine." This surprises me so I ask him about it later.

"I figured it out right around the time the Black Bandit was throwing a knife through my head" Schrodinger tells me. "You see, no one else knew Ghettoblaster was hiding Hammerspace, and I had long suspected Doom Machine of having some sort of ulterior motive. You do know he's not of this Earth, don't you?"

The fact is that no one seems to know exactly where Doom Machine comes from. Obviously he isn't from Earth because we don't build bipedal androids with rocket thrusters, hidden super lasers, and sentience here (or do we?). The interesting bit is that The Schrodinger doesn't seem to think he's from another planet either.

"He's from fourth dimensional space," the ancient supervillain elaborates. "I don't understand quite what that means. I've never been the scientific sort, but I heard him say something about it once. Malo told me Doom Machine was built by creatures from outside normal space and that was why he never trusted him."

Hammerspace chimes in. "The, uh, CIA guys got really weird when I brought up the whole lizard people theory."

"What, like on V?" says White Knight.

"What's V?" asks the Smiley Face Killer.

"Some terrible sci-fi show that was on before you were born," answers the Salesman.

"I just remember I made a crack about lizard people and they said something about four dimensional whatchamacallits," Hammerspace adds.

The Schrodinger remains skeptical. "The idea of highly advanced lizard people is a bit much even for me. I suppose we can't rule anything out though."

Our exit from the prison is considerably easier and less dramatic than our entry. With the guards fighting the inmates and the entire facility a raving mess of racial hatred, we simply walk out. The Hammerhead touches down outside the prison and the team climbs aboard.

On the jet I point out for the first time that the Fiendish Five now has six members and I ask if they plan to change the name. "I think we can keep it how it is," says Hammerspace as Fumigator passes him a martini. "The Ben Folds Five only had three guys and they were awesome."

The Schrodinger gives Hammerspace the coordinates of Doom Machine's lair and the two of them put together a plan for an assault later in the day. They tell me it's important to keep the element of surprise. Something tells me this will be far more difficult than this morning's raid on the supermax facility.

CHAPTER EIGHTEEN

"What we're planning here is an underwater insertion from a submarine," explains Baron Hammerspace as he sits in a leather seat inside Miley Cyrus's old Gulfstream jet, which he has rechristened Hammerhead. "With Doom Machine's secret lair being in the middle of the ocean, we're going to have trouble coming in via air without being spotted. The Schrodinger has a sub and we think that's the best way to remain undetected. Plus, it will be just like the beginning of Metal Gear, which is awesome."

The plan has come together only hours after the raid on the Supermax facility and the Fiendish Five are on their way to The Schrodinger's submarine. Smiley Face Killer reads a first edition Edith Wharton novel at the back of the plane while White Knight snores loudly with his head thrown back over a seat. Hammerspace, Fumigator and The Schrodinger continue to go over charts and blueprints while the Salesman sits next to me watching CNN on a small television.

The top story of the day is the legalization of not just marijuana, but also cocaine and methamphetamines, which was tacked on as part of the recently passed social equality bill. Under the new law anyone can use those substances and will be provided with them free of charge as long as they are within the confines of a government work camp. The intention is to take some of the strain off of the prison system, while simultaneously putting a lot of undesirables to work doing something constructive. So far it appears successful and volunteers are lined up in front of Job and Family Services centers all over the country waiting to board buses to the camps. I can't complain about anything that gets a few crack heads off the street.

We board Schrodinger's submarine at a harbor in France somewhere. The sub is dark and cramped. It is manned by a hundred henchmen and captained by Skullface, an old acquaintance I've heard Hammerspace mention a few times. Skullface gets his name from the massive white skull tattoo that takes up most of his face. He hasn't shaved in months though, and his giant beard looks ridiculous growing out of a painted skull. He wears an old Navy jacket, I think to signify him as the captain, but it's clearly something they picked up at a flea market. He smokes copious amounts of marijuana at all hours of the day and even when he's engaged in some sort of captain's duties he has a joint hanging from his mouth. The guy is perpetually high, and although I want to avoid him for that, I feel obligated to spend some time with him because of his shocking smoking chum: Osama bin

Laden.

"I didn't do it!" bin Laden insists, his eyes blood shot and surrounded by puffy red circles. He stuffs his mouth with a handful of cheddar cheese Bugles before continuing with his mouth full. "It was George Bush and Doom Machine."

"Argh! He always does this" says Skullface, like a pirate.

"Stop talking like pirate. You are not pirate, my man" bin Laden launches back. "I know pirates. I fund pirates in black sea. You know nothing about pirates."

"You know what we should do? We should break a tail light and drive all the way across the country with it busted and when a hot chick cop stops us, we can hit on her."

"The bullshit you say when you are high. Man, is bullshit. Is like you don't think at all. You want the pussy? You can have a wife. I have four. I share with you, my man."

So you aren't responsible for 9/11?

"No. I've been telling people that shit for a decade, man" bin Laden tells me. "George Bush did it! He wanted to attack Iraq!"

But you're not from Iraq.

"Think about it, man. If I am being from Iraq then it would be too obvious. He knew that. Think about it. The story does not work, man. Everybody is knowing the buildings had explosives planted inside. That was controlled demolition."

Then why did they fly the planes into them?

"That was to look scary. The planes was empty anyways."

The planes were empty?

"Yeah, man. Those people got money from George Bush. They're all living in Paris now. And they didn't even crash a plane into the Pentagon, that was a missile they said was a plane."

So George Bush blew up the buildings the same time he had empty planes crashed into them for no good reason and then he blamed it on a country he didn't care about so he could attack another country that had nothing to do with anything?

"Yes."

I don't believe him, but I've seen a lot of truly ridiculous things lately, so I give more consideration to it than I should.

"The truth is I am not such bad guy. You know, I like happy puppies and listening to jam bands and 8-bit Nintendo and death to America and watching *Grey's Anatomy* and puppies. Did I mention puppies? I am nice guy like you."

What was that thing before *Grey's Anatomy*?

"8-bit Nintendo? I love Nintendo. Is so much fun."

What disturbs me the most is that I hate him for being the kind of zombified pea-brain that watches *Grey's Anatomy* a little bit more than I hate him for wanting to kill me and everyone I know. I can't stand people that watch that show. I hate that they seem to believe it isn't just a mindless soap opera. It is. I assure you. It is.

"I am so high right now, man."

I duck out after a few minutes, hoping to avoid having the acrid odor of pot smoke cling to my clothes. Disappointingly, I fail at this. I find Hammerspace in the submarine's engine room with Schrodinger. He's excited.

"We just talked to Dr. Malpractice," Schrodinger tells me. "He says Power Team, Black Bandit, Ultra Guy, the Scarlet Avenger, The Crusaders and The Magician just stormed the GCL's lair looking for Hammerspace. They had a brawl with the whole Global Crime League. It's a crossover! This is fantastic!"

Baron Hammerspace seems less enthused.

The crossover, as was explained earlier, is the penultimate goal of every supervillain, just below actually dominating the entire world. A crossover occurs when a villain does something so horrendous or ingenious or horrendously ingenious that many superheroes who don't normally act together must join forces and cooperate to defeat him. The thing about the crossover that no one wants to admit is that the crossover is usually less of a means to an end and more of an end. As the stakes grow and the number of superheroes amasses, the villain gains more and more street cred amongst his peers. Villains become legends over night if they cause a big enough crossover. A lot of villains who claim to want world domination are really just trying to turn heads with a really spectacular super battle. All you have to do is apply a little logic to see that. How did El Malo Grande think a giant dinosaur monster was seriously going to help him subjugate all of the civilized nations? It didn't even respond to voice commands.

"Look, I'm not saying I don't care at all" Hammerspace clarifies. "It's cool and everything. I just don't want people thinking that's what I'm all about.

SUPERVILLAINOUS!

I'm in it to win it. Just ask Jose Canyousee. Oh, wait. You can't - because I smoked his ass on my way to world domination. If we're ever going to get to the next level of this thing then we need to stop doing more stuff like that and cut back on this grandstanding mano y mano brawl crap a little. That's all I'm saying."

CHAPTER NINETEEN

The underwater insertion into Doom Machine's secret base is not anything like the one in Metal Gear. The Fiendish Five, along with Osama bin Laden, and myself are packed into a tiny submersible vehicle which is old and rusted in areas. I can see areas of the hull which have been patched with welded metal plates. These appear to cover actual rust holes, not damage from any sort of weapons or missiles. I'm not sure which idea I find more worrisome, the possibility of missiles coming through the hull or just the rust.

I'm sandwiched between the White Knight and Osama because White Knight claimed the terrorist smelled like curry and someone needed to get between them.

"I can't stand next to the brown menace that's destroying my country behind my back," says the White Knight. "I took a vow long ago, when I put on this sacred robe, to defend my Aryan brothers from the plague of racial impurity and devil worship. I will not join hands with that darkie." On my right, the White Knight continues to prattle on about the secret brown conspiracy with the Jews to destroy the white man. On my left, Osama bin Laden rambles about the secret white conspiracy with the Jews to destroy the brown man. I suppose they have one thing in common.

The Schrodinger shushes everyone when we get close to the undersea base, which is an impressive glass dome on the ocean floor. "We must be careful not to make too much noise. They will be listening."

Hammerspace is marginally impressed by Doom Machine's lair. "The underwater dome thing is a little cliché, but it's pretty cool when you see it up close. I have to give it to Doom Machine for this one."

The supervillains find a place to sit down on the ocean floor next to the dome and they open a hatch on the bottom of the submersible. The Smiley Face Killer and The Salesman begin drilling into the earth with some pretty heavy equipment. Before long they've made a tunnel underneath the dome wall.

The villains hop into the tunnel and crawl through. I follow behind them. Doom Machine's dome covers a whole compound of a dozen or so buildings of different sizes. There is no pavement and we stand on ocean soil. This deep down there is no light from the surface, but the outside areas are lit by simple lamp posts. It looks like the gaslight district of some upper class urban neighborhood down here. It doesn't make sense to me that the ground is open. It seems like water should come up through the soil and get into the dome, but I'm no geology expert.

The Schrodinger leads the way into the closest

building, which looks like a massive airline hangar. I ask him how he figured out the layout of the compound. "You always build the giant super weapon in the biggest building. Where else would you put it?"

Inside the building we head down a dark hallway and that's when we come across the first of them: Doom Machine's henchmen. At first he has his back turned and he looks like a guy in a black business suit wearing a bowler hat. I notice the tail poking out under his suit jacket first, but I don't say anything because I think the supervillains are on top of this. The Smiley Face Killer creeps up behind him to take him out. At the last second, he turns and Smiley Face gasps. Doom Machine's henchmen are the lizard people.

The lizard man is about six feet tall and covered in green scales. Crescent shaped eyes peer out from under his black bowler and a mouthful of razor sharp teeth hiss. His hands have four fingers and those end in wicked talons. He has a long prehensile tail.

Killer regains her composure after a split second and goes Mike Tyson all over the lizard guy's face. He crumples to the floor. Hammerspace, who had been carrying a big shotgun, takes a good look at the beaten lizard man and pulls an elephant gun from his jacket. He hands another one to the Schrodinger, who accepts it while shaking his head in disbelief – never taking his eyes off the reptilian. He gives me a small snub nosed .38 revolver. I ask him what I'm supposed to do with it and he says "I'm all out of elephant guns."

The supervillains are slightly dismayed at the appearance of this creature. The Salesman pokes its face with the muzzle of a grenade launcher. "This thing looks pretty nasty," he says.

"Well, this puts a damper on things," says the Schrodinger.

I'm a little surprised by the reactions I'm hearing. I was under the impression that strange creatures were standard fare in this field.

"Molemen, yeah. But lizard people are bullshit," explains the Fumigator. "They're suppose to be bull-shit. Guys like George Noory made up lizard people so they would have something to do a radio show about at night. They aren't supposed to be real."

Oddly, the Fumigator is right. There are multiple occasions on record where molemen came up from the ground in gas powered drilling vehicles and attempted to subjugate small towns, although they only appear in groups of five to ten and are never particularly organized. There are several reports of them working in cahoots with human villains. They have left behind primitive weapons, photographs, and corpses. No one has ever produced any such evidence of lizard people.

"White Knight, does your superpower work on reptilian humanoids?" asks Hammerspace.

"Nope, jes white guys," answers the White Knight — something everyone knows already, but doesn't want to hear.

"There goes our whole plan," says the Salesman. "What now?"

Hammerspace makes the decision to go forward. "The Chaos Engine is right here in this building. I don't see much of anyone guarding it. One lizard guy isn't going to scare me out of taking over the world.

We're going ahead. We sabotage the machine and get the hell out of here just like the original plan."

We run a little farther down the hallway and it lets out into the giant main hangar area. The hangar is dark, and the villains begin arguing over whether they should turn the lights on or not. That's when the lights flip on by themselves and reveal two things: The nearly completed Chaos Engine – a humanoid robot that stands fifty meters tall even sitting on its butt, and a gaggle of about twenty lizard men pointing machine guns at us.

Doom Machine emerges from the surrounding gang of lizard people. "Welcome, my pets. I see you've finally arrived!"

"It's a trap. How did he know we were coming?" says Hammerspace.

Doom Machine replies "It's an underwater dome, you incompetent wretch. We can see everything coming for miles."

"Yeah. I was wondering about that on the way here," says Fumigator.

"You couldn't bring it up then?" says Hammerspace.

"To the death room with them!" yells Doom Machine.

CHAPTER TWENTY

"She just nagged the crap out of me all the time,"
says Hammerspace, sitting on the cement floor of the
death trap chamber. "The thing that really pissed me
off – and I still don't understand it – is that AFTER
we got divorced she bothered me more than when we
were married. You think you're done and you can finally wash your hands of something and it just keeps
coming back. It was constant. She would show up
and bother me while I was working and just create
drama. I would go to a bar with some guys and she
would just appear out of nowhere. I remember this
one time I was at this place on Spring street talking to
this hot little red head and I'm about to close the deal
and – BAM! There's Linda out of nowhere and she
starts yelling at me and calling this girl a slut."

After catching us sneaking into his giant hangar,
his lizard henchmen brought us to this large chamber
with metal walls and a cement floor. There is a large
drain in the center of the floor, which The Schroding-

er examines calmly. The Salesman is certain we are all going to die in here. Why Hammerspace has chosen this particular moment to detail the collapse of his marriage is absolutely beyond me.

"I remember another time I was breaking into the Metropolitan Art Museum with Iron Mongoloid," the Baron continues. "This was early on - I didn't have a costume yet – I still thought that was a bit much. We were using a jackhammer I borrowed to smash through the wall at night so we could go in there and load up. Then here comes Linda. She followed me there so she could blame me for the milk in her fridge that went bad. I swear to you that's why. I couldn't make that up. I told her I was trying to work but she wouldn't listen. We ended up zapping her with Mongoloid's trisomy ray and she just sort of wandered off talking about cheeseburgers. The effects are only temporary though."

Iron Mongoloid recounted the story for me later. "I made mean lady not smart," he told me.

For Melvin, the intrusions were becoming too much to deal with, especially when they hit him in the pocketbook. "I kept having to steal more and more to support these enormous alimony payments and they weren't even accurate. How the hell did they think a standardized test scorer made so much money? And it was like a vicious cycle because I would have to steal to make the payment and then because I could make the payment she would file suit for more money. She was trying to break me! And Dick Morgan was doing a hell of a job helping her."

Because of the skyrocketing payments to his ex-wife and ever mounting legal fees, Melvin could no longer keep up with the rent on his apartment. After six months of separation from Linda, Melvin was evicted. "It turns out that a place to stay is the one thing you just can't steal no matter how much infinite matter you can stuff into your pockets. It was somewhere I had sworn I would never end up again and there I was. It was ugly. It wasn't as bad as eating roaches back in Michigan, but it was bad."

Desperate for a roof over his head, Melvin turned to his only friends at the time, other young supervillains. "When you're new in the business you kind of look out for each other. A lot of new guys just coming split the rent on places. Bunk up. You go to auditions together when somebody's looking for a new minion. That's how it is. So I was crashing with this guy they called The Cape and he was a big costume guy. He had this twenty foot cape and an opera mask and all the old clichés - stupid stuff no one does anymore. Anyway, that got me thinking about costumes and throwing around ideas and The Cape started showing me his old comic book collection and then it was on. At the time I hadn't really come up with a solid name. I was using Captain Jacket, and Pocketman - which was a stupid name, looking back. The Cape was the one who told me about cartoon characters and hammerspace. That was when I came up with the name, the purple costume, everything – the whole persona. That was how I got into comic books too. Before that, I didn't read comics. I didn't really know what supervillainy was until then. Well, I found out what it is, but I hadn't really become it yet."

The Cape, now an English teacher at an unnamed east coast university, had this to say. "Yeah, we used to crash and I showed him all that stuff. That was years ago. I think I helped him create the image and the personality. The menacing language, the scheming – I showed him those things, but he took it and ran with it but he didn't really cross the line until the night – well, I don't know." The Cape is reluctant to say more, even after I pry very skillfully. Hammerspace is less secretive.

"Oh yeah. He's talking about the night we were at the Brooklyn Bridge fighting the The Peace Patrol," Hammerspace tells me. "They were this up and coming superhero team everybody thought would be hot shit. Me, The Cape, and The Chain Smoker had formed an alliance and taken out all of the power on this one street, because we couldn't figure out how to take down the whole grid, and Peace Patrol came to stop us. So we were all fighting on the bridge, because that's where you have super fights if you want to get noticed – on some kind of landmark. The Chainsmoker is getting his ass beat by the bald headed one with the machine guns for arms and The Cape is taking on two of them at the same time. I'm in the middle of stomping this guy who shoots ice from his fingertips with a flamethrower and a riot shield and I hear somebody's shrill voice screaming my name. I look back and there's [expletive] Linda. She hauls off and gets between me and the ice guy and starts screaming at me about how she's been checking my AOL account and she knows I've been chatting with some whore."

What he did next surprised everyone, and although many New York villains have heard some version of the story, few know the details. "I set the bitch on fire," Hammerspace tells me emphatically. "I had never killed anybody. It was all small time robberies and whatnot before that. But what the hell else was I supposed to do? She was there all the time, getting in my way, taking my money, making my life a living Hell. I was done with it. I pulled out a can of gasoline from my jacket, wet her down real good and then I lit her up like a bonfire with one of Chain Smoker's cigarette butts. She was keeping me down and that's what a villain does. He destroys whatever is keeping him down. It doesn't matter if it's a thing or a person. Villains don't care. We don't care. We will kill you if you get in our way."

The Peace Patrol ran from the bridge at the sight of Linda's burning form. "I just kept shouting at them. 'You want some of this?! You want some too?!' Nobody ever saw them again. It was epic."

The Cape elaborated more in a second interview by phone a few weeks later. "That was the night that he stopped being evil and started being EVIL. That was when he stopped being Melvin and really became Hammerspace."

CHAPTER TWENTY-
ONE

Being trapped in a death trap chamber is one of the strangest experiences I have ever had. I can't honestly say there is anything truly frightening about it, because most of the time I don't really believe the death trap (whatever it may be) is actually going to work. Other than the Salesman, the supervillains with me are largely undisturbed. Hammerspace has spent most of the time reminiscing about his misadventures, while the Schrodinger has carefully examined every square inch of the room. I think my composure comes from the simple logic that if Doom Machine really wanted to kill us he would have done so much earlier, rather than placing everyone in this elaborate mechanism.

"Yeah. That's the thing about death traps. They never really work," Hammerspace says. "Guys use them because they're classic and showy. It's like people who build hot rods. It's not like you're gonna drive that thing to work every day. You get a Nissan Altima for that. It's a much more practical car."

The Schrodinger is equally calm. "I haven't a certain idea what this contraption does, but I have it narrowed down to a few possibilities. I'm confident we'll find some manner of escape," he says. "The problem with death traps is that, while normal humans would meet certain doom in them, superheroes have super powers for which cannot be accounted before hand. The more super people you put in a trap, the more likely some combination of skills that will allow escape. I should know – I've made that mistake more than a few times." He sneers and chuckles in snobby evil fashion.

Fumigator elaborates. "The classic death traps are the walls closing in (with or without spikes), the room that fills with water, the pendulum room, the pet monster eats you and all of its variants including mutant fish, lions, tigers, velociraptors, tentacle rape mutants, and a great white shark (with or without cybernetic modifications)."

"Don't forget the tree lynch and the road haul," adds the White Knight. "Them are the only death traps where I come from. Works every time."

"I've tried them all at one time or another," says Schrodinger. "Nothing could be less effective than the pet monster trap. That is, by quite a distance, the worst."

Hammerspace agrees. "Yeah, superheroes beat up armies of dudes with guns on a regular basis. There's no way they're going down to a bear or a tiger or whatever. I haven't done much deathtrapping myself, on account of my money situation."

Can't you steal pretty much anything you want?

"Sure, but you don't get pet great white shark wealthy stealing TVs and selling them. You need to make investments, buy real estate, stuff I've never been good at."

Right about then the walls start to close in. They come at a snail's crawl of a pace, so slow it's not immediately obvious that they're moving. The Salesman becomes extremely flustered. The White Knight curses a lot. The Smiley Face Killer tries pushing on the walls to no avail. Fumigator only rolls his eyes and Hammerspace laughs.

The Schrodinger scoffs. "I was figuring on this or water filling up the room to drown us all – what with the drain and everything. I suppose that's just for easy clean up. After we're all crushed they can come in and hose everything down the drain."

Hammerspace pulls an anvil out of his jacket and sets it in the center of the room. He sets another one next to that. Pretty soon he has a stack of them about six wide and four tall. Once the walls hit the anvils they begin to creak.

"This is exactly the kind of thing I was referring to earlier," says The Schrodinger. "How could Doom Machine ever predict anything this ridiculous?"

The walls, unable to crush the stack of anvils in the center of the room, eventually they give way and we hear a loud blasting noise as whatever mechanism propels them bursts somewhere in an adjoining chamber.

After this, Hammerspace uses a concrete saw to cut through the wall and lead us out of the death trap chamber.

All of this begs a simple question: Why didn't Doom Machine take Hammerspace's jacket away?

"I have no idea," Hammerspace says.

"You think that's bad?" interjects Schrodinger. "I once forgot to take a multi stage plasma rifle away from The Disciplinarian. He melted a whole pit full of acid spitting lava snakes and then he said – I'll never forget it – 'Looks like you need to sit in time out and think about what you did.' Then he kicked me into the pit and left me there. He killed all the guards and left with the last jeep! I was in the middle of the amazon rainforest! It took four weeks to walk to the nearest town!"

"I let some kid keep his pocket knife once," adds the Smileyface Killer. "He thought I didn't know about it. I still killed him." She shrugs.

"One time at terror camp, I was torturing American journalist and he concealed handgun and he did not to how to work safety! Oh my Allah. Was so funny," says bin Laden. "I pulled his fingernails out with pliers. So funny."

"Okay, everybody listen up," Hammerspace halts the discussion. "Osama bin Laden, you and Mike Leon go with White Knight to fire up the submersible."

White Knight disagrees. He refuses to work with a "raghead" and risk muddling his racial purity. Hammerspace restructures the marching orders. Then the Smileyface Killer complains about being left alone with a racist. Salesman says White Knight is more of a bigot than a racist. Then an argument breaks out over the definition of racism. Hammerspace mixes up the teams again. Finally, The Schrodinger and Osama bin

Laden are going to power up the submersible, while Hammerspace, Smileyface Killer, White Knight, the Salesman, Fumigator and myself head for the main hangar to plant explosives on the Chaos engine. The teams split up.

The base is unusually quiet on the way back to the main hangar. There are no lizard men to be seen and we see nothing in any of the rooms we pass as we make our way through the corridors.

When we finally reach the main hangar again, the lights are turned on and the hangar is empty. Completely empty. There is no chaos engine. There is no pack of lizard men waiting for us as a trap. There is nothing at all.

"Shit. They're gone," says Fumigator.

"Not all of them," answers the evil metallic voice of Doom Machine as he levitates down from the ceiling high above us. "I remain."

"This is a pathetic trap, Doom Machine. Give yourself up now and perhaps we will spare you a slow death!" shouts Hammerspace.

Doom Machine laughs. "Ignorant cretins."

"You don't stand a chance against all of us, dimwit," says Killer. "I'm gonna enjoy taking you apart."

"Perhaps..." answers Doom Machine.

And then the last thing anyone expects happens. The room is flooded with superheroes. Black Bandit, Power Team, Fire Dancer, Captain Commando, and a bunch of superheroes I don't know smash their way in through walls, doors, hatches, air ducts, vents — everything a person can fit through and few things they can't. The clamour of pithy one liners fills my ears from every direction. Just when I think they're going to start smashing Doom Machine to pieces, the Scarlet Avenger emerges from the crowd of heroes.

"Good job, Doom Machine," she says. "Now we can finally bring these evil doers to justice."

CHAPTER TWENTY-TWO

"Wait a minute. What?" says the Salesman to the army of super heroes standing in the middle of Doom Machine's secret underwater hangar. "You guys are working for Doom Machine now?"

"No, you fools," answers Doom Machine. "Doom Machine is no more. From now on there is only Peace Machine, and I'm one of the good guys!"

"Uh. Peace Machine sounds really lame," cracks Hammerspace.

"It does lack a certain catchiness," chimes in the Scarlet Avenger.

"It's a pussy name," the Salesman grunts emphatically. "Sounds like something a hippie paints on the side of his van."

"I second that," says the Smiley Face Killer. "What about Fortune Machine? Use an antonym to play on the role reversal."

"That sounds like it dispenses Chinese cookies."

As I'm standing in the middle of this massive empty hangar now filled with superheroes, three things occur to me in exactly this order. One: This conversation is ridiculously stupid (like Doom Machine's new name). Two: I could be seconds away from the all-out super battle I've wanted to see this whole time. Three: I really need to hide from the Scarlet Avenger.

I try to slip behind the Smiley Face Killer at first, but then I decide the White Knight will probably obscure me better with his giant robes and all. It's too late anyway. She sees me.

She scowls angrily. "You! You tramp bastard! Give me one reason not to tear off your massive and perfectly formed manhood and use it to box your ears!"

I'm at a loss for words. Usually I just walk away from women when they get like this, but I'm pretty sure that isn't an option here.

"How could you? You think you can just walk out of someone's life after you make unforgettable and passionate love to them for hours and hours - well past the endurance of any normal man. You think after bringing a woman to dozens of the most earth shattering climaxes of her lifetime using your unmatchable skill and experience as a lover that you can just walk away?"

This is all quoted word for word. I swear. I don't take any liberties with my reporting. That would be grossly unprofessional.

"Whoa! You hit that?" exclaims the Salesman. "Mike Leon is a pimp!"

"I am not a WHORE!" screams the Scarlet Avenger.

"Hush it up, toots," the Salesman says as he reaches into his jacket pocket for a tiny little plastic bag. "How about you take this dime bag of dick cheese to go sit in that corner for twenty minutes?"

The Scarlet Avenger enthusiastically takes the dime bag of (apparently) smegma back to the corner of the hangar and leaves us all alone.

The Salesman elaborated in a later interview. "I always keep a little bag of it for when I really want to bring somebody down. I think that's what pushes the envelope as far as it can go. I could have a dog turd or something, but that's kid stuff. Dick cheese is original. Dick cheese really makes a statement."

It doesn't take much after that for the whole room to slide down a slippery slope into total chaos. The Black Bandit steps up in the Salesman's face and yells at him for disrespecting. The Smiley Face Killer tries to break it up. Fumigator talks some smack to Commander Commando. The tipping point is when Peace Machine cries havoc (literally he screams, "havoc!") and zaps White Knight with some kind of molecular destabilizer. The White Knight explodes all over most of us, a big pink bloody mess.

I look around for somewhere to hide in the empty hangar, but there is none. This is just one massive empty square room. All around me, heroes and villains are doing battle. Hammerspace throws grenades at the members of Power Team, as Smiley Face Killer swings Ms. Frigid into Bullet Time like a giant baseball bat. The Fumigator runs circles around the room spraying toxic gas at heroes I recognize and some I don't. The Salesman smokes a cigar next to me.

"This is a losing battle, kid," he says, picking a bloodied unidentifiable chunk of White Knight out of his hair. "I guess we are all the same on the inside." Just then, Black Bandit bashes him in the face with a gloved fist. Hammerspace quickly pounds the bandit with the Mallet of Malice and sends him sprawling.

"We're getting out of here!" the baron yells. "Go! Go! Go!"

He doesn't have to tell me twice. I'm running down the tunnel to the outside faster than a crackhead catching a bus. Salesman and Fumigator are right behind me. Hammerspace stops at a door and waits for Smiley Face Killer to push back the hordes of heroes. Then he bars the door with a lead pipe and they keep moving.

"Doom Machine booked it as soon as the fighting started," yells Fumigator.

"I noticed," Hammerspace replies. "He probably figured they would finish us off."

"He almost figured right."

"Good riddance. The guy was a racist douche bag," says Smiley Face Killer.

We're back at the submersible in record time where the Schrodinger and Osama bin Laden are waiting for us with the engines fired up. As soon as Killer seals the hatch we're on our way out and water begins pouring into the undersea dome through the hole we cut to get in. I'm not sure how the super heroes will get out, and I don't care. This was entirely too close.

CHAPTER TWENTY-THREE

It's been two days since the huge mess at the undersea secret base of Doom Machine. In light of recent events, Hammerspace and friends have spent the last forty-eight hours in hiding from any sort of super people. Hiding is pretty easy for supervillains, as they essentially just remove their masks and mix in with the general populace. For the Schrodinger, Smiley Face Killer and the Salesman, things are a little more difficult as they don't really have secret identities. They've gone to live with Osama bin Laden, whose vanishing act is legendary throughout the entire industrialized world.

I don't want to talk too much about the villains' secret identities, as that might compromise them, but I will give some of the bland details. Contrary to popular myth, Osama bin Laden does not live in a cave. He lives underneath the ball pit in a play place at a popular restaurant in America. I will not specify which restaurant.

The inside of his bunker is concrete and mostly unadorned. There is very little furniture and only some simply metal shelves for storage, though there is plenty of extra space. The place is minimalist at best. He does have wireless internet access (hijacked somehow from a neighboring establishment) and there is a small television, although it only gets twelve channels on a good day.

I'm sitting on a throw rug that I found stashed in a cardboard box on one of the steel shelves. I've been elected to go out for supplies once a day, because I am the least recognizable of the group. This means I have to climb up a ladder and open a secret hatch into the tube maze. Then I make my way through the maze past half a dozen stinky, slimy children. I hate children. They're loud and messy and they ask annoying questions. The sound of them shuffling around in thousands of plastic balls above us never ceases. I can hear it right now. It is quite obnoxious.

Osama and Smiley Face Killer are having an argument I can't believe I'm hearing. The boredom is clearly already getting to them.

"Is tearing up his heart when he is with her? Then he does not like her," bin Laden says.

"No, because he says when they're apart he feels it too," she answers, heatedly. "No matter what I do I feel the pain, with or without you."

"Eh, does not make sense. His heart hurts with her. Hurts without her. Has nothing to do with her I think. He needs go to doctor. He has medical condition."

"It's a song. It doesn't have to make sense."

"No. Should make sense."

"It was the nineties. Nothing made sense in the nineties."

"Backstreet Boys made sense."

"WHAT?!!!?"

"Just saying. That is all. Just saying."

It is a little after noon on the third day when Hammerspace makes an appearance. He climbs down the ladder from the ball pit and makes an announcement.

"Assemble, my villainous, team of warmongering doom bringers! For, tonight, we ride into history!" he yells, waving the mallet of malice around like some kind of madman.

Later that afternoon the rest of us learn that "ride into history" means driving to Dayton, Ohio in a rusted Winnebago. Dayton is a carcass of a city no one should ever visit. In some ways it is like nearby Cincinnati, where I come from, but it is largely devoid of people. This has always confused me, as Dayton has somewhat more interesting attractions and up-scale establishments, including the finest strip club I have ever patronized, the United States Airforce Museum and one of the world's largest miniature wargaming facilities. Despite this, everyone lives in Cincinnati, which boasts no strip clubs, a useless football team, and several vacant shopping malls.

The Salesman parks the Winnebago outside a Buffalo Wild Wings on the campus of the University of Dayton. It is there, inside the RV, that we rendezvous with the remainder of the Global Crime League: Principal Uncertainty, Dark Pope, and Ghettoblaster.

Ghettoblaster is the most upset.

"Man, he blew up our shit!" he yells, as Dark Pope attempts to calm him.

It takes several minutes of listening in for me to catch up with the latest events, but it seems Doom Machine, accompanied by a cadre of superheroes, flew into the fortress of the GCL and destroyed everything overnight.

Now, weakened and divided (Mr. Meltdown sided with Doom Machine in the conflict) the GCL has turned to Hammerspace for help.

CHAPTER TWENTY-FOUR

"There's the glaringly obvious stuff that people see all the time," Hammerspace tells me as we walk down a cracked sidewalk in an empty warehouse district. "Everybody gets that evil monologues are stupid and death traps never work, but there are other more sinister things we could be doing that get overlooked. It's the smart stuff we don't do that screws us more than the dumb stuff we do do."

He pauses for a second. "Do do? Does that always sound funny to you? Is that even proper English?"

I'm not entirely sure. I think a somewhat liberal linguistics professor would say yes, but a proper tight-ass expert would tell you no. I don't really care personally.

Following Hammerspace, we turn into a dilapidated warehouse.

"One thing I noticed is all the big city waterfront abandoned warehouse hideouts. Those are too easy to find and we take a lot of ass beatings there," he says. "We still went with the abandoned warehouse, but this one is in the middle of nowhere – worse than nowhere – the Midwest. Out here I'm more afraid of church ladies than super heroes. They might think we're a cult or something if they see us in here."

I think it's more likely church ladies would assume some sort of gay orgy party before they jump to any satanic assumptions, considering the amount of colored tights I see in the room we've just turned into.

Inside the warehouse, at least seventy supervillains are crowded around the Fumigator asking questions about whatever Hammerspace has planned. He refuses to answer any questions and struggles to keep them all pacified. They all turn and stare.

I'm able to pick out some that I know. The Fiendish Four or Five are here, as well as the remains of the Global Crime League. Of the others I recognize Doctor Deviant in his impervious Malpractice Suit, Count Chocula, Road Rash, Freddie Mac, the Toxic Shocker, Skullface, Steve Jobs, Professor Punishment, the Man Eater, the Woman Eater, and Oderous Urungus from Gwar.

"Minions! The time draws near!" he screams. It echoes through the vacant warehouse. "Peace Machine has aligned himself with the pathetic super cowards in a bid to enslave us all and this world along with us! But his treachery will not prevail! For our treachery is far greater!"

The various costumed villains in the room seem

taken aback. There is a minor uproar when he refers to them as minions, but they are quickly subdued by the shooshing of the more well known supervillains.

"Fumigator! Prepare the presentation!" Hammerspace shouts, again shaking his fist wildly.

Fumigator hustles over to the nearest wall, against which an old rusty easel is propped facing away from the supervillains. He picks up the easel and unfolds the legs, setting it on the floor in front of him and spinning it around so that everyone can see. Attached to the front is a giant sized POST-IT™ pad. Written in poorly hand scrawled fat permanent marker across the top of the pad are the words PLAN FOR CONQURING THE SUPERHEROES.

"Wait, what?" Hammerspace says. "A giant size post-it? What happened to the Powerpoint presentation?"

"The Salesman couldn't get it to work," Fumigator responds.

"Where's the Salesman?" Hammerspace scours the room until he sees the Salesman. He motions a shrug and makes a bewildered face.

"We don't have a DVI to VGA adaptor for the projector," the Salesman responds.

"That's just great," Hammerspace chides angrily. "Do we at least have the little model city?"

Fumigator shakes his head.

Hammerspace buries his forehead in the palms of his hands.

A pirate themed villain called the Quartermaster steps forward from the crowd on his one peg leg. "Uh. You guys spelled conquering wrong."

Hammerspace glares at the Quartermaster. His

eyes bulge. "YEEEEAAAAAAAAAAAAAAAAA-AA!!!!!!!!!!!!!!!!!"

He pulls a huge gun from his jacket. It looks way too big for anyone to hold and fire with one hand. It has glowing and blinking lights flashing away all over its body and ends in something akin to a radar dish.

Hammerspace points the gun at the Quartermaster and pulls the trigger releasing a massive blast of super heated plasma energy across the room. He cackles loudly as the Quartermaster vaporizes in a screaming second.

For the first time since we walked in, the room is completely silent.

"Spelling? Spelling? No one cares about spelling! I don't care if we have to use an etch-a-sketch to make our battle plans. We will destroy the superheroes and that filthy coward Doom Machine along with them!"

He turns to Fumigator and shouts "Fumigator, show the battle plan!" As he brandishes his massive plasma gun in the air.

Fumigator nervously turns back to the giant POST-IT™ note. He looks back once at Hammerspace and uses a sharpie marker to insert the missing e in conquering. Then he flips the page.

The second page of the POST-IT™ displays a poorly drawn sketch of the White House. Fumigator explains. "Tomorrow morning at oh six hundred, a team led by the Salesman will kidnap the president's daughter from her Sidwell Friends school in Washington DC."

Hammerspace interrupts to demand a picture of the president's daughter. At his behest, a terrified Fumigator draws a stick figure on the POST-IT™

pad.

"She has long hair!" screams Hammerspace.

Fumigator draws long hair on the stick figure. He then looks back at Hammerspace for approval.

"Good. Good. Please continue."

Fumigator continues. "After we have secured the girl, she will be transported to the Paris." He flips the page again to reveal a marker sketch of the Eiffel Tower. "We will take her to the top of the Eiffel Tower, where she will be roped up and held for ransom."

He turns the page again and the next POST-IT™ shows a massive superfight occurring on and around the Eiffel Tower. This is drawn entirely with stick figures. "After the superheroes arrive to save the girl, we will ambush them with superior numbers and defeat them."

"We will crush them once and for all!" Hammerspace roars.

The crowd roars back. "Crush the superheroes!"

To me this plan sounds oddly reminiscent of many past plans to set a trap for superheroes, none of which were successful. After Hammerspace's display with the giant plasma gun, I'm not planning to say anything.

CHAPTER TWENTY-FIVE

The flight to Paris is entirely uneventful. I go it alone, figuring I'll meet up with Hammerspace and his team after they've done their business in Washington. I have nothing to do for the fifteen hours aboard the plane. I wish I brought my Game Boy. I play my Game Boy occasionally at home, but never anywhere else. This is because I don't want to be seen in public playing video games. I realized a while ago that this completely defeats the purpose of Game Boy and so I stopped carrying it with me.

I borrow a newspaper from the guy in 6C and he's excited about the top story, which is that the government is allowing illegal immigrants and anyone on government assistance to live on the work communes for free. They're levying a value added tax to help pay for that, but 6C says that will only affect people who are already making too much money anyway.

I skip through most of the paper and sleep for the rest of the flight. I hit the ground in Paris and within the hour I'm standing at the top of the Eiffel Tower with Hammerspace and Sandy Montgomery, the president's daughter. Having just missed the ransom demands*, I'm a little confused about a few things. What I know for a fact is that I'm very high in the air with an insane person screaming at the French down below and an obnoxious little girl tied to a steel beam. I don't like children. The following is a transcript taken from my tape recorder.

Sandy Montgomery: Do you think they're gonna kill me? They better not kill me.

Mike Leon: I'm pretty sure it's not in the actual plan, but who knows with these guys.

SM: Then what the hell do they want?

ML: Uh... Mostly street cred with other guys in spandex outfits.

SM: What?

ML: Street cred.

SM: What does that mean?

ML: Eh. You know. A rep with other bad guys. East coast west coast... Like, uh, like Ice Cube.

SUPERVILLAINOUS!

SM: The guy who makes all those family movies?

ML: No. Well... Yeah. Christ. What are you like fifteen?

SM: Sixteen.

ML: See back in the day, Ice Cube came up on the streets and he was all about handling bitches and smoking the chronic. But that was like when I was a kid.

SM: The seventies?

ML: Hell no! How old do I look to you?

SM: You have a receding hair line.

ML: This again? It's always been that way. It's called a widow's peak. It's a stupid name.

SM: You look like Dracula.

ML: Yeah. I dated a girl who called me Bat Boy.

SM: I think it makes you look like that guy from that stupid Japanese cartoon with the spikey hair...

ML: Vegeta? Yeah. I've heard that too.

Hammerspace: Silence! You're distracting me from looking out!

SM: Let me go, asshole!

Hammerspace: You. Girl. Have you ever danced with the devil in the pale moonlight?

ML: It's quarter after noon.

Hammerspace: I have jet lag!

ML: You're wearing sunglasses...

Hammerspace: Silence!

SM: Look, all I know is you better not kill me. Or rape me. And you better not throw me off of the space needle!

Hammerspace: <expletive>. This is the Eiffel Tower! And you go to private school? <expletive>. You're not even on the right side of the world. Wow.

SM: Whatever. My dad will give you money! As much money as you want!

Hammerspace: I want not money, child! My dream is one of conquest and glory! I demand to rule over the entirety of the world with a cruel and crushing hand so merciless it will make the Soviet Empire appear like a little pink pre-school. My war machine will grind to pieces any sad and pathetic resistance like so many bits of mulched grass ejected from the sprayer of a Lawn Boy self propelled zero turn radius mower set to SPEED SEVEN!!!!!

After that outburst there isn't much more conversation. In the few hours we've been up here, the French army has surrounded the perimeter and they've begun shouting up to us with bullhorns. Hammerspace yells back at them now and then, and at one point he pisses off the tower trying to hit a French tank. That turns out to be impossible because of the wind. One thing that intrigues me here is the lack of super attendance in general. I see Hammerspace, obviously, but no one else is around.

The first superhero to arrive on the scene is a French hero called Ze Duelist. He wears a beret and carries a white glove in his hand which has the peculiar ability to lash out and slap targets several meters away. He arrives via hot air balloon and smacks Hammerspace several times with his strange white glove, but this proves to be little more than a minor annoyance. Hammerspace pulls a gun on him and he surrenders. He only speaks French, but the international language of being a pussy is pretty well understood by all. Hammerspace shouts "Today, I take NO PRISONERS!" and then he shoots Ze Duelist in the guts and kicks him over the railing.

Another hour goes by before real superheroes touch down on the tower platform. When it does happen it is truly a sight to behold. Well, as much a sight as any of the crazy shit I've seen on this assignment.

The first to hit the observation deck are the flying superheroes. Led by the Scarlet Avenger, a cadre including Lightning Guy and The Flying V lands on the platform looking particularly angry. Behind me, the Black Bandit appears from a puff of smoke. Before he can say anything gruff and edgy, an elevator load of non-flying superheroes gets off on the deck. In seconds, the Power Team and all of their super friends have Hammerspace on the observation deck.

"I'm gonna mess you up," says the Black Bandit.

"Careful," says Scarlet Avenger. "This has to be some kind of trick."

"It certainly is, Vomit Projector," Hammerspace growls. "You have all come here to meet your doom!"

And with that, he tosses a briefcase sized metal box from his jacket. It clanks to the grating at our feet as he screams "Vortex, now!" Instantly, a super villain I've never seen before (Vortex, I assume) flashes into existence behind Hammerspace. He grabs the baron and the two of them vanish into thin air.

"It's a trap!" says Admiral Ackbar.

"Dammit, Hammerspace," screams the Avenger as she leaps for the case. "Bandit, is this what I think it is?"

"It's a Russian suitcase nuke," responds the Bandit. "RA-115, 6 kiloton yield. I can disarm it, but I need the case open."

"Done," says the Scarlet Avenger as she tears the locked metal case open with her hands. Even a few superheroes flinch. Frankly, I'm amazed no one shit their pants.

The Black Bandit goes to work on the device and his hands move like Carlos Santana's across the neck of a fine Gibson guitar. He disarms the bomb quickly and when he's done he spins the open case around so everyone can see the timer frozen with only three seconds to detonation.

"Impressive," remarks Commander Commando. "It's too bad the news cameras didn't get that."

That's when the Scarlet Avenger turns her attention to me.

"Oh. Mike Leon. I feel like I haven't seen you in ages. So, how are things? Are you still working on writing stories or whatever?"

I tell her yes.

"That's great. Good for you. You know, Peace Machine and I love stories. We read stories together all the time. You know Peace Machine, right? My boyfriend?"

I turn around and he's there. Doom Machine. Peace Machine. Whatever the hell they're calling him now. The Scarlet Avenger is at his arm right away. I'm immediately confused. I thought Doom Machine was a robot.

"Finally somebody says something," says Wombat. "I've been thinking about it all week!"

"Yeah," agrees Bullet Time. "How do you guys, you know?"

"That's none of your business!" growls the Avenger.

"But he's a flippin' robot!" says Wombat. "Robots can't have sex."

"Data banged Tasha Yar on Star Trek the Next Generation," says Bullet Time.

"That's a TV show."

"So?"

"He's fully functional," says the Avenger, smugly caressing Peace Machine's arm.

Everyone cringes.

"So does he have a metal robot dong?" Wombat asks.

"That doesn't make any sense. He's an alien robot. Why would aliens give him a dong?"

"I told you. He's fully functional."

Everyone cringes again.

"SILENCE FOO-" says Peace Machine. "I MEAN, PLEASE BE QUIET.... PEOPLE. WHERE HAS HAMMERSPACE GONE?"

Indeed, where has Hammerspace gone? The lack of supervillains present here is disconcerting to say the least. According to Hammerspace's plan there should be an army of costumed baddies whipping the shit out of all these superheroes. Of course, nowhere in the meeting did I hear anything about a nuclear bomb being tossed at my feet either.

"He figured that bomb would kill us all and he left," says the Scarlet Avenger. "It's what supervillains do, Sweetie."

It's impossible to tell if Peace Machine believes what the Avenger says by the unchanging appearance of his indestructible alien metal face, but I don't think he does.

And by the next morning, we all know far too well that she was wrong. The whole world knows that she was wrong.

Hammerspace's now famous ransom broadcast included demands for all American currency to carry the phrase "In Baron Hammerspace we trust" and that Selena Gomez drink the blood of a virgin calf to be sacrificed live on the Disney channel. It can be seen on Youtube.

CHAPTER TWENTY-SIX

In the morning the superheroes are dead. Well, most of them anyway.

It happened like this: After the Eiffel Tower incident the heroes stood around for some time posing for photos with the President's daughter and taking questions from the press. Despite Peace Machine's insistence that they all stick together and hunt down Hammerspace's villainous super gang, the heroes all parted ways to fly back to their various solitary sanctums and black caves and shitty studio apartments. None of them noticed they were being watched.

Using an array of spy satellites and robotic insects provided by the Global Crime League and their nearly bottomless resources, Hammerspace's team followed the heroes back to their homes. Only a few of them were lost in the trek (and they still remain out there to this day). After learning the heroes secret identities and living arrangements, the villains had every advantage.

They struck in the night, in teams of at least three for the less threatening heroes and as many as ten for the stronger class three costumed crusaders. And so fell most of Earth's superheroes – not locked in titanic struggles against giant mutants and maniacal madmen, but blasted to death in their sleep by creeping bad dudes with deathly death lasers of death.

Why supervillains have not done this before is a subject of much speculation. It was easy to do and didn't require large sums of resources. It certainly wasn't a problem of ingenuity either, considering comic book nerds have been bringing up the idea for at least fifty years. I venture to say after my experiences that the explanation is psychological – that most supervillains would rather feed their own egos by battling in costumes in front of screaming onlookers than actually achieve any sort of result. Hammerspace is a little bit different of course.

Now the villain sits here in his command station, the corner booth of a McDonald's in Los Angelos, underneath a wall mounted television set to Fox News Channel. Across the restaurant, another television shows CNN. He tells me he likes this spot because it's quiet so he can hear the TV. Also, they have the best hot mustard. None of the restaurant employees seem surprised that a guy in a purple costume has been here for hours eating fries and constantly checking his Blackberry smartphone - probably because this is L.A.

"We had guys stationed in all the major cities already waiting so we could coordinate all the attacks at roughly the same time," elaborates Supreme Overlord of Evil Hammerspace, after declaring himself the Supreme Overlord of all Evil super entities on earth. "We had to do it all as quickly as possible so they didn't have time to figure out what was happening and assemble some kind of counter offensive."

The plan was carried out with diabolical precision and ruthless aggression. There were remarkably few casualties amongst the evil-doers although a few high profile losses were unavoidable. Most notably, Principal Uncertainty was killed and survived in Los Angelos and Washington respectively and irrespectively. He will be forgotten and remembered.

"I would say the MVP for the night goes to Skullface," Hammerspace tells me. "He whacked the Black Bandit by tossing a plastic explosive in his shower. Then he imploded the apartment building where Laserbooster and Ninja Girl live. Funny thing. They lived two doors apart on the same floor of the building and we're pretty sure they didn't know about each other. What are the odds?"

"We had a lot of trouble getting to Power Team, given their living arrangement inside a giant fortress plaza, but we did get Commander Commando. The asshole was alone at a movie with a fifteen year old girl! Somebody call Chris Hansen, right? No, seriously. What a sicko. He's trying to take advantage of a baby. So then he sees our guys, Salesman, Gunninator, and Ultra-Killer, and the jerk grabs the little girl and tries to use her as a human shield! What is wrong with this guy? What ever happened to chivalry? You know? He's a super hero for God's sake."

So what happened?

"What do you mean what happened?" he emphatically replies as he glances at his Blackberry. "Gunninator blasted them both to mince meat and score one for the bad guys. His guns are huge. Have you seen those things?"

Isn't shooting teenage girls a little overkill?

"Wow. Captain Obvious is on fire here."

I think it's a valid question...

"No. No. Captain Obvious is really on fire, right here," he says as he spins around his phone for me to see. "Dark Warlock just posted the pics on Facebook."

Indeed, Captain Obvious is burning. He has been tied to a pyre and set ablaze by Dark Warlock and Flaming Queer, as proven by the pictures on Hammerspace's phone. I had no idea there was an actual Captain Obvious.

"Yeah. He's minor. In and out of a few B-list teams. He never had much going for him on the super power front."

Still there were some failures. "Turns out you can't kill the Scarlet Avenger," the Supreme Overlord relates. "At least not any way we can figure out. Smiley Face, Domimatrix, GeForce, Pokey Man, and Count Chocula ambushed her in a Starbucks. They beat her ass for at least two hours. They broke that bitch – I mean broke her. And she still wasn't dead. They're pouring concrete over her out in New Mexico right now. We figure if we can't kill her we can at least bury her for a decade or two."

Then something happens that terrifies us both. Both TVs in the room cut to static. Then Doom Machine appears on the monitors in close-up. He growls robotically.

"GREETINGS HUMANS! AS YOU NO DOUBT HAVE LEARNED BY NOW, THE WORLD'S SUPERHEROES HAVE BEEN SLAUGHTERED IN THEIR BEDS IN AN IN-GENIOUS DISPLAY OF TRICKERY AND TAC-TICAL BRILLIANCE ORCHASTRATED BY ME!"

"What?! No he didn't!" yells Hammerspace. "I killed the superheroes!"

"WITHOUT THOSE SUPERPOWERED CRETINS TO PROTECT YOU, I DOOM MA-CHINE, DECLARE MYSELF RULER OF YOUR WORLD! NOW, HUMANS, COWER BEFORE THE MIGHT OF MY CHAOS ENGINE!"

And with that, Doom Machine shifts the camera up to display the hulking metal Chaos Engine, acti-vated and fully operational in the middle of Times Square.

"That son of a bitch!" screams Hammerspace. "He's stealing the credit for everything I did! I'm sup-posed to be evil ruler of the world!"

He boils with rage as he leaps up from his seat. "Come on, Mike Leon. We're going to New York."

CHAPTER TWENTY-SEVEN

When Hammerspace said we were going to New York, I thought he meant on a plane or perhaps in a car. I had no idea he was talking about teleporting there via Vortex's dimensional rift opening capability. Tearing through space/time is like doing somersaults in the cockpit of an F-16 while the plane does barrel rolls. When we materialize on the top of a tall building, I quickly learn the answer to every question I've ever entertained about the physics of vomiting off of a skyscraper.

He hits the roof and he's already on the move. The whole way down fifty floors of stairs he's cursing. "God damned Doom Machine. Stealing credit for everything I did! Can you believe this crap?"

Also he built a device that's going to destroy human civilization.

"Yeah. There's that too. But what really irks me is

the whole superhero thing. He was disguised as a superhero to hide from me! Not to kill them. That was MY MASTER PLAN! That sorry son of a bitch. When I find him I'm going to shoot him right in the god damned face with a molecular destabilizer. I don't care if he is invincible. I'm gonna curb stomp the bastard's balls. I'll jam the biggest gun I have straight up his ass and pull the trigger until it clicks!"

When we reach them bottom he still doesn't stop. The streets are packed with thousands of fleeing city dwellers. Hammerspace walks against the flow of screaming foot traffic. A few yards out of the building Vortex drops off Fumigator next to us and then the Smiley Face Killer appears from an alleyway. As the explosions grow louder, so does our entourage of supervillains.

Before long, we have fifteen or twenty villains with us. Hammerspace is still continuing his vicious monologue of all the horrible things he plans to do to Doom Machine once he sees him. The terrified pedestrians have thinned out quite a bit. The ground rumbles harder and the crashing sounds of metal smashing concrete grow louder. Hammerspace keeps getting louder and louder too, to stay audible over the destruction happening only a few blocks away. Fumigator leans over and shouts at me.

"The noise is what always surprises people at these things. It's like a Metallica concert, but louder!"

Finally it is so loud I can tell we're very close. We turn a corner and there it is. The Chaos Engine. Standing upright it is much taller than before and I can make out its features more clearly now. It is blocky, but vaguely human looking. It is steel colored and appears unpainted. Black and yellow cables are exposed in a few places, but most of it is heavily armored. Its feet end in massive metal talons rather than toes. The talons curve downward and stab into the concrete whenever it takes a step. Its legs bend twice, once at the knee and then again before the foot, like a bird or some kind of hooved mammal. Its body is more heavily armored than any other part of it and behind the body extends a long tail which sticks out straight as if to balance the whole mass and ends in a behemoth laser cannon of some type. The arms are small compared to the rest of it and each of them is equipped with a four Vulcan cannons like the ones on a Spectre gunship. The head sits on a skinny neck and forms into an elongated maw filled with shining razor like teeth. Looking down at all of us, it opens its maw and roars!

"Holy crap! It's a big robot dinosaur!" exclaims Fumigator as he stares upward into the mouth of clanking metal destruction.

"INDEED, FOOLS," says Doom Machine floating above us. "STARE INTO THE GAPING MAW OF YOUR DESTRUCTION!"

Hammerspace shouts back waving the mallet of malice in the air. "No, YOU fool! Stare into the crushing metal mallet of YOUR destruction!"

"THE CHAOS ENGINE IS SEVENTY METERS OF COMPLETELY INDESTRUCTIBLE DESTRUCTIVE POWER, ALL CONTROLLED BY AN INSANE COMPUTER! YOU HAVE NO CHANCE OF SURVIVAL, HUMANS! NOW DIE!"

Doom Machine's shoulder pads slide open and a

bevy of heavy artillery erupts from inside his armored shell. This includes several small rocket launchers and at least one multi-barreled heavy machine gun. He zeroes in on Hammerspace and the chaingun roars to life.

Hammerspace snatches an old woman as she runs past us and uses her as a human shield. Hundreds of bullets shred her to pieces. He then tosses her to the ground cackling evilly. "It's good to be bad!"

"CHAOS ENGINE! DESTROY THEM!!!!!!!!!!!!!!" Doom Machine bellows.

Fumigator punches me in the shoulder. "You should get clear. Shit's about to get real."

But all too quickly, shit does get real. Really real. Incredibly ridiculously real. The Chaos Engine whips its tail around and fires its laser cannon in our direction. Villains scatter. I hug the concrete. Before I can stand, the engine is already snapping down on the street with its massive steel jaws. It takes a bite out of the asphalt underneath us like someone biting into an apple. The teeth miss my arm by a few feet and I see Dark Warlock crushed between two twenty foot molars. He dies screaming in a popping, squishing, explosion of red gore that squirts in all directions. Some gets in my eye and it stings, but I run like a chickenshit school girl anyway, figuring I'll blink it out when I get behind a building or something.

I have no idea where Hammerspace has gone. He may have been eaten by the Chaos Engine. I don't even know where I am. Just that I ran blindly for the nearest structure. I rub my eyes and shake my head. I peek around and see the Salesman standing next to me. We're under the giant glowing Bank of America sign on the corner of the Marriott Marquis building. The Salesman yells. "We're screwed, kid! It takes like ten superheroes to fight Doom Machine when he doesn't have a giant robot dinosaur with him!"

Maybe you can sell the robot something?

"Like what? The Iloveyou virus? Are you <expletive> retarded, kid? Seriously. Did Iron Mongoloid zap you with the retard beam?"

Our exchange is interrupted when Gunninator sails between us, pitched out of the melee going on in the street by some unseen and extreme force of violence. His bulky blued steel frame smacks the Salesman's hand as he rockets past us and crashes through the glass storefront of the Bank of America behind us.

"Shit!" the Salesman hollers. "I jammed my God-damned finger!"

Gunninator struggles from the wreckage of the storefront coughing and sputtering. He's sliced up pretty badly from the broken glass and a few small shards of it remain stuck in his skin. "How did I get over here?"

"Doom Machine threw you," replies the Salesman. But Gunninator topples like Sonny Liston, face first into the concrete before he can register the answer. The Salesman rolls his eyes. "I can't sell anything to robots and I'm pretty sure you can't kill them with derived and unoriginal writing. Both of us are worthless here. We need to go."

I agree, but first I duck down and grab a .45 automatic from Gunninator's arsenal. The Salesman winces. "What the Hell are you gonna do with that?" he says. "You might as well throw paper clippings at them."

Just then, an M1A1 tank rolls by the Marriot building. The Salesman screams. "Go now! Use the tank for cover!"

The second we charge out from under the sign, the tank is smashed into the pavement by the giant hammering tail of the Chaos Engine. The Salesman curses and stops short of getting crushed along with it.

The tail whips back up into the air and then changes direction to come back down on top of us. I close my eyes. There is an immense smashing sound and when I uncover my face, the Smiley Face Killer is standing in front of me, straining to hold up the behemoth metal tail.

"Run!" she grunts.

The Salesman, white as a ghost, does nothing. I punch him in the shoulder and he startles to action. We both dash across the street, narrowly avoiding another tank. We are running in the general direction of the Virgin sign when he says "I think I shit myself." He checks. "Yeah. I definitely shit myself."

We're almost to One Times Square when someone reaches out from behind a box office booth and grabs me. It's the Schrodinger. He's wearing an army jacket and carrying a backpack full of explosives. "You two, come here!" he says.

The Salesman stops. He shrugs. We follow the Schrodinger around to the side of the Bowtie Building where Domimatrix is huddled on the ground in front of a laptop computer. She wears her hair in a green and black striped Mohawk that matches her leather fetish wear. Her black bustier is encircled by a belt of handcuffs.

"Domimatrix has been using a packet sniffer to try and decode whatever signal Doom Machine is using to control the Chaos Engine," Schrodinger shouts. "But I fear she's making little progress."

"This is like no encryption I've ever seen before," she interrupts.

Behind us an M1 tank fires its 120mm cannon. It sounds like a child's balloon popping compared to the stomping of the Chaos Engine.

I ask Schrodinger what happened to Hammerspace.

"He and Vortex are trying to lure Doom Machine into a stasis mine on top of One Times," he tells me.

"Isn't that where they drop the ball on New Year's?" asks the Salesman.

"Yes."

"So if you stop time up there, won't it stay the same year forever?"

The Schrodinger and I both ignore the Salesman's unbelievably stupid question. He draws his own conclusion.

"Wow. Now Dick Clark really is gonna live forever."

"None of it makes sense. It's like the code is just gibberish," Domimatrix growls, frustrated.

"Doom Machine said the Chaos Engine is controlled by an insane computer," Schrodinger says. "That simply must mean something."

"I thought all computers were already insane," says the Salesman.

"Computers can't be insane. They're just a series of switches. Ones and zeroes. They can't be crazy," says Domimatrix.

"Broads are all crazy too. A crazy broad telling me computers aren't crazy? I'm pretty sure that means they're crazy."

The Schrodinger cocks his head at Salesman's comment and turns to Domimatrix. "He might be on to something there."

"Excuse me?" she says, offended.

"Sane people think crazy people are crazy, but to the crazy the crazy are sane."

"Right now I think you're crazy."

"What if the ones are zeroes and the zeroes are ones?"

Domimatrix raises one eyebrow. "I guess... That could... Yeah. Yeah. That's it. Give me a minute with this."

Just that second, Vortex materializes nearby with Hammerspace in tow. Hammerspace carries a stinger surface-to-air missile launcher. He screams up angrily at an unseen Doom Machine somewhere in the sky-line above us.

"You're like that fat kid that copied off my third grade spelling test! You know what happened to him?!" Hammerspace screams. "He got detention!"

And then Hammerspace takes aim and launches the stinger from his shoulder. Again, it makes barely any noise compared to the ongoing commotion. I don't see if he scores a direct hit or if the missile veers off into the stratosphere, and Hammerspace doesn't stick around to see either. Vortex grabs him and they vanish into some unknown passage of space/time just as the blur of Doom Machine's rocketing form stabs a fist through the empty air where Hammerspace's face just was. Doom Machine growls and his rocket boosters thrust him back into the sky and away from us. Only the discarded missile launcher remains as evidence of what just happened.

"That was close," says the Salesman. "Maybe you guys can use that to shoot at the dinobot."

We ignore the Salesman again. Even if those missiles were reusable, they would do nothing to penetrate the Chaos Engine's armored hide.

"I've got it!" exclaims Domimatrix. "I'm in!"

"About time," the Salesman quips. "Oh, shit!"

The Chaos Engine leers around the around the corner staring down on the villains and myself. A 120mm shell smashes into its face, which it soundly ignores. In its right hand, it grips the crushed cadaver of Skullface, which it dumps a few dozen storeys to splatter on the ground at the Schrodinger's feet. The Schrodinger draws something akin to a World War Two era stikkbomb from his backpack. "I was saving this," he says.

"Is that a thermal detonator?" shrieks Domimatrix.

He doesn't stop to answer. He just charges at the Chaos Engine's left foot. The robot rears up and stomps on him, smashing him into the New York city street and leaving a footprint the size of several school buses.

"We should run," says Domimatrix, picking up her laptop.

She barely has time to turn around before there is a white flash and the Chaos Engine's left foot erupts in a flaming mushroom cloud that rises a hundred feet off the street.

"Holy shit," the Salesman says, running next to me. "Those aren't supposed to exist!"

You learn something every day.

Looking back, the thermal detonator has done some good. Most of the Chaos Engine's foot is a shredded mess of jagged steel and hanging cables. Sparks shower from broken electrical connections down to the street below. The machine moves forward stabilizing itself with its tail as a crutch. The Schrodinger was able to at least slow it down.

"I don't get it!" Domimatrix yells. "I keep sending it the deactivate command, but it just keeps coming!"

We pass a Buick LeSabre full of Ghettoblaster's henchmen shooting at the Chaos Engine with Mac-10s and Uzis. The Salesman shakes his head at their ignorance as a giant fist smashes the car to metal scrap. None of them survive.

With the same hand, the Engine picks up the car and throws it at a flying supervillain I can't recognize. The car slams into that villain and continues until it passes out of view behind the surrounding skyscrapers.

"We're running out of bad guys," says the Salesman. "You getting anywhere with your computer hacking skills, lady?"

"I told you," Domimatrix scolds. "I'm sending it the deactivate command!"

"Are you sure that's not the kill Salesman harder command? Because that's what it looks like!"

"That... Wait. That makes sense!"

Domimatrix taps one-handed on her laptop and then mashes the enter key.

The Chaos Engine stops in its tracks. The streets

grow quiet as its turbine engines slow their spinning to a crawl and then cut off entirely.

"It's an insane computer. It does everything backwards!" she says. "I sent it the activate command."

The Salesman roles his eyes. "Do I have to do everything?"

"Something smells like shit," she replies, sniffing the air.

The Salesman quickly changes the subject. "Wasn't this thing supposed to make everybody on the planet fly into a murderous rage?"

"Or something," says Fumigator, as he approaches from behind a shattered battle tank. Most of his alligator muzzle has broken off and now his mask forms a strange looking model of an alligator's uvula, including a neat cross section of the last two or three inches of jaw before the throat.

"You look like I feel," says Salesman.

"Where's Schrodinger?"

"<expletive> robot stepped on him," Salesman flippantly responds.

"The lasercannon almost took my face off," Fumigator says, pointing to his sliced off alligator mask. "It picked Smiley up and threw her to – I don't know – Alaska or something. We're down a lot of guys and Doom Machine is still flying around here somewhere."

A quick survey of the landscape proves him correct. I can see the remnants of dead supervillains and bystanders strewn about the square. Rubble is scattered on the sidewalks, mostly fallen from buildings above. In the place where the Chaos Engine first took a bite out of the street, the subway underneath is now exposed. Occasionally, a terrified citizen or two dart from a doorway and run off down the deserted street, but other than that, there is no activity on the square. It appears that those in immediate company are the last remaining supervillains on the scene.

That's when Doom Machine chooses to drop in and visit us. He lands on the street with his back turned to us, staring up at his motionless giant robot. He then turns and glares at us.

"WHAT IS THIS OUTRAGE!?!?!?" he roars, pointing an accusing finger. "YOU! YOU HAVE DONE THIS!"

Before anyone can move, Doom Machine's shoulder mounted missile launcher fires off a rocket that screeches directly into Domimatrix's chest. A second later, I'm standing next to a disembodied pair of legs wearing leather knee-highs. There was no explosion. It made no noise. It looks like the space where she was standing simply vanished.

Fumigator throws a smoke bomb down at his feet and disappears into a spreading gray mist.

"This is bad," Salesman says. "Real bad."

Behind Doom Machine, a block down the street, Vortex and Hammerspace blink into existence. Hammerspace levels a large soviet sniper rifle at Doom Machine's back.

Something, maybe a facial tick, maybe a reflection, maybe the sound of Hammerspace's shoes against the pavement, maybe the smell of gun oil — something gives them away.

Doom Machine doesn't even turn around. He shoots some kind of death ray, mounted on the back of his head, at Vortex and zaps him into a smoldering heap. I can't hear Hammerspace from this distance, but I can see him glance down and curse.

"I GROW TIRED OF THIS FOOLISH GAME, HUMAN!" Doom Machine bellows.

Hammerspace raises his rifle and takes a shot, but the bullet flattens against Doom Machine's armor and clanks to the street in front of us.

"We're screwed," says the Salesman. "Totally screwed."

"I WILL PUNISH YOU WITH MY FISTS, FOOL! PREPARE TO MEET YOUR DEMISE!" Doom Machine growls as his boosters flare and he rockets toward Hammerspace.

Hammerspace doesn't even have a chance to react before Doom Machine picks him up into the air and hurls him what is easily one hundred feet into the Salesman. Both of them roll along the ground and slide to a stop crumpled underneath a massive poster for *Spiderman: Turn off the Dark*.

At this point I crawl under the broken M1 tank nearby. Standing around in plain sight of an angry Doom Machine doesn't seem like a good idea. Looking through the spaces between the wheels holding the tank's treads in place, I can see Hammerspace attempting to stand. He doesn't look good.

Doom Machine lifts off the ground and rests his hands on his hips, in a show of truly diabolic splendour. "I WISH TO TAKE THIS MOMENT TO THANK YOU, HAMMERSPACE. BY MURDERING EARTH'S HEROES, YOU HAVE MADE MY JOB MUCH EASIER! BY THIS TIME TOMORROW, THE CHAOS ENGINE WILL BE RE-

PAIRED, AND THEN IT WILL RAMPAGE ACROSS YOUR PRIMITIVE CIVILIZATION UNCHECKED, CRUSHING YOUR CITIES IN ITS GIANT METAL JAWS, SLAUGHTERING YOUR ARMIES WITH ITS BEAM CANNON, AND STOMPING ON YOUR CHILDREN WITH ITS GIANT INDESTRUCTIBLE FEET!"

"And a sound that makes everyone on the planet fly into a murderous rage," the Salesman says, dazed not getting up from the ground.

"Yeah. What happened to that?" Hammerspace adds.

"WHAT?" Doom Machine asks, surprised.

"It makes a sound that causes everybody on the planet to go crazy."

"NO IT DOESN'T."

"I was told it did that." Hammerspace searches the ground. "Where's Mike Leon? Mike Leon, didn't those guys – you know the guys - tell me that?"

I yell back from under the tank. They told him that. I have it on tape.

Doom Machine scratches his chin. "CURIOUS."

"If it doesn't do that, then what does it do?" the Salesman asks smugly, propping himself on his elbows.

"IT HAS DOOM LASERS AND EXPLODER MISSILES AND A BEAM CANNON! AND HUGE FEET FOR STOMPING!"

"So you just ripped off El Malo Grande's idea?"

"HE STOLE IT FROM WATCHMEN!"

"Do you just steal everybody's work or do you actually come up with anything original?" Hammerspace interjects.

"HOW DARE YOU ACCUSE ME OF BEING UNORIGINAL IN MY MANIACAL PLANNING! YOU STOLE YOUR PLAN TO KILL THE SUPERHEROES FROM AMAZING SPIDER-MAN!"

"Oh, really?"

"YES! THE GREEN GOBLIN DID THE SAME TH- WAIT. WHY AM I ARGUING THIS FOOLISHNESS? I SHALL DESTROY YOU AND YOUR PLANET NOW. NONE MAY STAND IN MY WAY, BECAUSE EARTH'S MIGHTIEST HEROES ARE ALL DEAD!!!!!!!"

"Not all of them," Hammerspace says, reaching into his trench coat.

Doom Machine doesn't make facial expressions, but somehow he appears confounded. His head cocks to the side slightly and then rears backward as he sees what's coming. The seconds seem to crawl by in slow motion as a red, white and blue blur emerges from Hammerspace's coat, drawn by his gloved purple hand and hurled in the direction of Doom Machine.

"GENERAL WELFARE?" Doom Machine sputters, as the invincible superhero smashes into him appearing equally confused.

"Doom Machine?" he replies.

For a brief moment the two of them simply stare at each other, not having any idea what move to make. Then General Welfare turns and sees the Chaos Engine and the demolished New York streets.

"Doom Machine!" he says, clicking to full awareness. He punches Doom Machine in the face.

BOOM! The sound of the General punching Doom Machine echoes through the streets. BOOM. He hits him again. BOOM. BOOM. BOOM!

"I'll teach you to kill my sidekick and destroy Philadelphia with a robot crocodile!" General Welfare shouts, obviously disoriented from living in Hammerspace's jacket for so long. "Take this! And that!"

Neither of them sees Hammerspace as he slinks away.

Minutes later, I crawl out from under the tank to see Doom Machine lying in a crumpled heap, his armor cracked and chipped, his slightest movements making a labored whirring noise.

"That's what you get for being evil, Doom Machine." General Welfare says, standing over his shattered body.

"You should probably finish him off," the Salesman sputters.

"No, Salesman. Killing is wrong," General Welfare says. Then he looks around again, curiously. "Now, how did I get here?"

I help the Salesman up, and he lights a cigarette.

"Best crossover ever," he says.

AFTERWORD

No one knows what mysterious forces guided Hammerspace in his rise to power, or why they lied to him about the Chaos Engine. The badly broken Doom Machine was hauled away by the army after the super battle in Times Square and we will never know what secrets he took with him. As for the strange lizard people helping him build his ultimate weapon, they vanished as quickly as they appeared.

The super community remains in disarray. Most of the superheroes are dead because of Hammerspace's efforts, and the villains were nearly all slaughtered in New York. Ghettoblaster was vaporized by the Chaos Engine's tail cannon. The Schrodinger hasn't been seen since he was crushed under a giant foot. Mr. Meltdown was eaten along with a big chunk of city street. Gunninator is still in a coma.

A few survived to continue their craft. The Smiley Face Killer regained conciousness somewhere in

Northern Arkansas, where she began a violent rampage that lasted for days. Fumigator fixed his mask and went back to doing exactly what he was doing before the crossover. General Welfare remains a heroic beacon of truth, justice and the American way. He's leading a public effort to find and excavate the Scarlet Avenger from her concrete tomb. He called me asking questions, but I told him I couldn't help.

Still, others simply moved on. The Salesman quit the life and got a job at J.P. Morgan. Dark Pope converted to Hindi. Wombat married a movie star and opened up a chopper shop.

Hammerspace, of course, keeps on soldiering away. Determined to rebuild the Global Crime League with himself at the helm, he plots away in his Fortress of Evilness in his (now native) Evilonia, a tiny province in Eastern Europe. He sits on a lavish leather couch with his feet up, his spiral bound notepad at hand. A fire crackles in the hearth and talking heads blabber on a giant plasma television.

"I'm pretty sure Dark Pope is out, but Smiley is in," he tells me, jotting something down in his notepad. "I came up with this thing where we'll sneak mind control hypno messages into Harry Potter audio books that tell kids to steal all their parents' money and mail it to us. I think it's solid."

As for me, I've had as much supervillainy as I can handle. I have been shot at, teleported, trapped in a crushing machine, thrown out of a plane and nearly crushed by a skyscraper sized robot. I had a one-nighter with an unstable super heroine. I traveled all over the world and saw the inner sanctums of legends and the hidden lairs of maniacs. I learned all about the importance of a cool name, and a costume to go with it. I watched Hammerspace rise from a nobody in a studio apartment to a world class threat with his own country.

Despite all of it, I can't help the feeling that I've learned nothing. I still don't understand why they put themselves through all of this. The schemes they concoct rarely amount to any serious gain. Most of them don't even make sense. At best, some superheroes show up and they have a loud and theatrical fight whilst terrifying a lot of people. This crossover was amazing, but what was it all about? Doom Machine wanted what? To smash some buildings and make a lot of noise? He couldn't have seriously assumed he and his robot could seize control of the entire world. Could he? Hammerspace likely has a billion dollars worth of military munitions in his jacket, and yet he's planning to have hypnotized children mail him grocery money. Why? Isn't it all a lot of sound and fury signifying nothing?

On the TV, a panel of experts argue over the President's announcement this morning that he is forming a special new wing of the military under the social equality act. They replay the footage of his announcement.

"...and I think it's time for Americans who believe in freedom, to stand up for that freedom. We need to make sure people who don't think like us aren't walking around weighing down the rest of us."

The crowd in front of him cheers.

"And that's what the Social Equality Requisition Forces will do. They're going to make sure that certain problem people are put in the work camps, where they can lead productive and happy lives, instead of causing problems for people who work every day, and further more, we're going to be extending the work camps so that anybody can go join them. You can volunteer to go there and we'll feed you. We'll clothe you. We'll take care of you. All for just an honest day's work."

The crowd cheers louder this time. The President breaks from talking to smile and put his arms in the air.

Hammerspace shakes his head.

"Look at this do-gooder," he says smugly. "It's guys like him that really just don't get it. Here he is, talking about saving the world, and what does he do? Make a speech and sign some papers? What's that going to do? He doesn't even have a costume!"

Indeed. He does *not* wear a costume.

If you enjoyed this book, please leave a five-star review on Amazon and tell all your friends. If you don't, I might end up working for the phone company and wearing a plastic name tag for the rest of my life.

ABOUT THE AUTHOR

Mike Leon lives at the heart of Cincinnati in a 100 year-old shack of a house where he takes a 9mm pistol to bed like a teddy bear every night. His sense of humor is darker than a homicide detective's but not quite as dark as a serial killer's. He likes yeast donuts with chocolate frosting. Also kittens. He likes kittens.

also by Mike Leon...

BUY IT NOW OR THEY'LL
KILL YOUR KIDS.